TRAPPED

TRAPPED

PAMELA BUCHANAN

ARPress
45 Dan Road Suite 36
Canton MA 02021

Hotline: 1(800) 220-7660
Fax: 1(855) 752-6001

Ordering Information:
Quantity Sales. Special discounts are available on quantity purchases by corporations, associations, and others. For details, contact the publisher at the address above.

Printed in the United States of America.

ISBN-13   Paperback   979-8-89356-094-7
                      eBook   979-8-89356-095-4

Library of Congress Control Number: 2024904583

CHAPTER

1

After speaking from my heart and providing Derrick with my real feelings. I could see from the expressions on his face. That, he never really knew I felt this way. Yes, I have always felt trapped in a marriage that seemed to be going nowhere. My marriage repeatedly reminded me of a demolition ball being thrown into the structure of a building in which the bricks would come tumbling down without knowing where they will land. Not only have our structure in this marriage been knocked down, but it has left me wondering when Derrick will show me who he really is. Funny thing is, he has been showing me for years. It has just been me refusing to see what was right in front of me. Truth be told. I was the one who needed to see themself and refrain from blaming oneself for another's faults. Instead, I would just cover up his behaviors and act like they never happened. Therefore, I stopped asking him to show me who he was and just let him be. I got tired of him putting on a show for me.

I can recall Aunt Rose telling me once before, that if you want Derrick as your spouse. Don't allow him to be your child. If you want him as your best friend. Don't allow him to be a frenemy. Whatever you ask Derrick to show you. Just make sure you can show him the same and can accept what he shows you. But if you are in denial of who you are. You will surely be in denial of what he will show you.

So, I'm trapped in my mind, my heart, and even my soul. All because, I accepted others treatment and even my own treatment of denial. Looking over at Derrick right now and reminiscing about what Aunt Rose stated. I wanted him to respond, but he remained silent. I guess my words were still floating in the room, because we all were like sitting ducks with our beaks shut tight. This silence was present for a couple of minutes. I guess the doctor was even giving us a moment to process what he had just shared.

"Mr. and Mrs. Wilson, I will have my nurse set up future appointments and I will also have her provide pamphlets on HIV. They will give more information about the disease and provide available support groups in the area. You will also receive a call from the health department. They usually reach out to further assist those who may not understand the disease and provide recipients with free services. Are there any other questions you all have for me at this time?"

Responding first I blurted out, "No, I don't have any further questions!"

"Neither do I. I just got to process all of this. First, I get shot. And now I'm being told I am HIV positive! This hurts worse than being shot." Derrick explained.

"Well, look at it this way. You now know what you did not know. If you would not have been shot. We may have never known you were HIV positive. "I stated in a strong voice.

We both got up and exit the doctor's office. As we strolled quickly to the car. The tension between us was at an all-time high. Arriving to the car, Derrick opened my car door and shut it behind me. He walked over to the driver's side and got in. After cranking up the car, he turned on the radio. What a coincidence that a song, Lean on Me, by Kirk Franklin was playing on the radio. Listening to this song play as we drove off. Some of the lyrics became stuck in my mind. All I could hear were the lyrics:

> I am here.
> You don't have to worry.
> I can see, your tears.
> I'll be there in a hurry when you call.
> Friends are there to catch you when you fall.
> Here's my shoulder, you can lean on me.

With tears beginning to roll down my face. I turned to see if he noticed me crying and I was shocked that his face was as full of tears also. This made me cry harder. Derrick reached over and grabbed my left hand. We rode in silence continuing to listen to music. Then, I noticed Derrick was on a different route than the one we usually took to get home.

"Derrick, where are we going?"

"I think we both need some fresh air. And at this point, I need to be close to the one that have always mattered besides you."

"This looks like the way to the cemetery. Why are we going out there to get fresh air? We could have gone by a park!"

"Passion, I just want to visit my son's grave. Can you please just be patient with me on this? I promise after this. We can go home!" Derrick said with a groggy voice.

Entering the cemetery gates, I became so nervous. Derrick and I never really came out here together. Therefore, I'm on edge of why today. Derrick pulled up to the section of where Derrick Jr. was buried. Before he got out of the car. He turned and asked me, "Would you like to go with me?"

"I guess. I haven't been out here in so long!"

Derrick continued his performances for today of being a gentleman by opening my door and helping me get out of the car once more. As we walked to Derrick Jr.'s grave. I couldn't help but look around the graveyard. For some apparent reason today, it seemed quieter than normal and incredibly beautiful. There were rose bushes in some areas. Different flowers planted in others. And even had some small trees sprouting up. As I continued to admire the scenery, we finally reached his grave. The headstone stood upright in marvel granite with a picture of him in the center. The word caption on the headstone read, "Gone too soon, but lives in our hearts forever." Derrick kneeled to embrace the headstone and began crying as he uttered words of regrets. Seeing Derrick kneeled in that position, reminded me of the day we received the call of Derrick Jr. being hit by a car. DJ was hit as he crossed the street from getting off the school bus. Ironically, we both had just arrived home from work when the phone rung and on the other end was Derrick Jr.'s mother Kevelyn screaming.

"Passion, I need Derrick Now!"

"Who is this?"

"Passion, I don't have time for the foolishness. This is Kevelyn! Something just happened to DJ!"

Without further delay I yelled, "Derrick, please get the phone! Something has happened to DJ!"

Derrick got on the phone. He spoke with Kevelyn for a few moments and then we left immediately. We proceeded to the location she provided, only to find a crowd of people everywhere. And as soon as we got out of the car, people started running up to Derrick trying to tell him about the accident. He wasn't trying to hear nothing anyone had to say at this point. He just wanted to get to his son. Arriving before the paramedics and the police gave us a disadvantage of getting through the crowd. Derrick finally grabbed my hand and maneuvered us through to the place DJ laid. Finally getting to such a unbelievable view. I spotted Kevelyn and her sister. Kevelyn's sister was embracing her while they looked at a lady performing CPR on Derrick Jr. Standing at a standstill, Derrick and I did the same. He really surprised me because he remained calm the whole time the lady performed CPR. It was not until the paramedic arrived and pronounced DJ dead that Derrick became erratic. He lost it. He began yelling profanity and punching in the air. It took three police officers to get him to calm down. After calming down, Derrick kneeled and embraced DJ in his arms kissing his face repeatedly. He had lost his only child after seven short years of living. All because two fools decided to race down a main highway and ignored the stop sign that intruded from the side of the school bus. The sad thing about it was the children on the bus watched it all happen and a little five-year-old girl was also hit. She survived her injuries and only had minor scratches on her body. Unfortunately, DJ sustained a broken leg, broken ribs, and a cracked skull. The impact was so hard against DJ that it knocked his shoes off his feet two miles down the road. After observing the scene of the accident. Everyone was left so devastated. Therefore, I believe on that day, a part of Derrick died with his son.

"Derrick, are you ok?" Watching him embrace the headstone.

"Yes, Passion. This is the only thing I can embrace to make me feel close to him. I guess I will be joining him soon!"

"Derrick, why would you say that? People live with HIV every day! Are you giving up or something?"

"I don't know what I'm going to do! I feel just like that day when I lost DJ. I am so fucking confused, angry, and I wish all this shit could just end Passion. But deep in my heart. I know it won't just because I want it to!"

Just as Derrick spoke these words. A red cardinal landed on the left end of the headstone and stared straight at him. We both looked at each other in amazement. Thinking back to an old myth our ancestors believed. A red cardinal appearing in your presence is a symbol of the gift God gave you and should remind you of the time you shared with your loved ones. You should also be thankful as well. From the look in the bird's eyes staring directly at Derrick and the loud chirping it was sounding off. Neither of us said a word. Derrick got up and wrapped his arm around my back. In awe, I couldn't take my eyes off the bird. Watching the bird in amazement. Tears traveled down my cheeks. We both had the strangest feeling that this bird represented DJ and he wanted to tell his Dad that everything would be ok. Therefore, I granted his wish.

"Derrick, everything is going to be ok babe! Thanks for bringing me out here. You were right. I needed this. I see things a little clearer now."

"P, I needed this too. That bird just gave me what I came looking for. I think now we can go babe!"

Derrick and I started to walk off and the bird chirp loudly turning in the direction we were walking. When we arrived at the car. We both looked back and noticed the bird had walked right behind us the entire time.

"Passion, do you see that?" Derrick asked.

"Yes, I do!" Placing my right hand on his face and gently kissing his lips.

"What was that for Passion?"

"I just want you to know. I still love you! Please be patient with me and give me time to deal with all this."

After I spoke this to Derrick. The bird flew away as though his mission had been accomplished.

"Thanks DJ! Daddy knew coming to see you would make everything better." Derrick said as he blew a kiss in the air to the bird. "Passion, you know that was DJ reincarnated and he is no longer below the ground. Our son is flying high!"

CHAPTER

2

We drove out of the cemetery and proceeded home. Once we arrived at home. I noticed a police car parked in front of the house. I immediately felt on edge as though I was the alleged shooter.

"I wonder what he wants now." Derrick stated in discuss. "I'm not ready to talk about it just yet."

Well, I guess you don't have a choice from the looks of it."

As we got out of the car, we noticed the officer was already waiting at the edge of the garage door. Derrick and I exited the car. I unlocked the door and turned off the alarm system before walking farther into our home. I didn't wait for them. I went straight into the den, because I knew that is where Derrick would bring the officer.

"Hello officer. How can I help you today?" Derrick asked.

"My name is Officer James. If you don't mind. I would like to ask you some questions." The officer responded.

"Yes, it's ok. Please come inside."

The officer followed Derrick into the house into the den. Derrick offered him a seat.

"Can we get you something to drink?"

"No Ma'am. I'm fine. I just want to ask a few questions and get out of you all's hair."

"So, what questions do you have for me?"

"I know you said before, you didn't know who the man was that entered the room. But can you give me some type of information on the person?" The officer asked.

"Like I told the other officers. He had on blue jeans, black tennis shoes, a ski mask, and a black hoodie. He appeared to be in his middle or late thirties. Looked to weigh about two hundred pounds standing at six feet tall. Oh yeah! I was able to see his wedding ring. It was a black and silver band. That's really all I can remember."

"Ok, is there any reason you can think of, that would make someone want to shoot you?"

"Well, there could be many reasons. But I can't pinpoint it down to just one."

"So, could one of the reasons be about the young lady, who accompanied you at that time?"

When the officer stated this. It brought anger back up inside me. I quenched my teeth, snared my nose sideways, and begun to roll my eyes.

"Possibility! But I am not sure." Derrick stated.

"Ok, so Mrs. Wilson. Maybe, you can tell me of any reasons you may know of? Especially, since you were seen leaving the crime scene?"

"I have explained my presence to the other officers. I will not answer any more questions. Until, I have my lawyer present!"

"Ok. But I'm just asking standard questions." Officer James explained looking at me side eyed.

"Maybe so. But I still want my lawyer present. Question for you now is, am I a suspect?"

"No, Ma'am. You're not. It is our protocol to ask all who may have been involved varies questions."

"Ok, thank you, but no thank you!"

I believe my sassiness may have angered the officer. Because he didn't ask any more questions.

"Well, I guess that's all of the questions for now. We shall meet again soon."

The officer got up and Derrick escorted him to the front door.

"Thanks for you all's time!" Officer James said as he walked out the door to his police car.

"Have a great evening, Sir!" Derrick said as he shut the door.

Derrick returned and stared at me. "Passion, what was that all about?"

"It was about protecting myself. I didn't do anything wrong, and no one is going to try and make it look like it."

"I just don't want you making them go after you for nothing!"

"Well, then you need to tell them who it is!"

"Ok, enough of that. We just got on a different level and we're not going backwards." Derrick stated.

"You're absolutely correct. So, do you care to join me in cooking dinner like old times?"

Derrick laughed and said, "You bet. Wow! It's been a long time since I heard that question."

We both laughed and went into the kitchen. I proceeded to take out the hamburger meat to make Derrick's favorite meal. He is a lover of spaghetti with a salad, and garlic bread.

"So, what are we going to prepare?" He asked.

"I thought we would cook your favorite meal." I laughed as I said it sarcastically.

"Oh, so we are making my favorite meal. Now, I really know going to the cemetery was a great idea." He said laughing while retrieving the onions and bell peppers from the refrigerator.

After placing the macaroni to boil. I put the ground beef in a skillet to cook. Since Derrick was chopping the onions and bell peppers. I turned to get them from him. As I turned, I ran right into him. He was standing closely behind me. We immediately embraced and started kissing. As bad as I wanted to embrace him back. I could not put my hands on him, because I still had grease on them from placing the ground beef to cook. But Derrick was able to place his hands on my back and pull me closer into him. I could feel his manhood rising, as well as my nipples started to extrude outward. This passionate kissing bought on feelings; I had not felt in a long time. We continued kissing for a moment, until I pulled back and glared into his eyes. This kiss took me back to the first time, he kissed me while we cooked together. There was no anger or sadness present in that moment. Just a reminder of how we once loved each other without trying to love others.

"Why are you looking at me like that?" Derrick asked.

"Derrick, I'm just wondering about our sexual life now."

"What do you mean?"

"Since my result were negative. I don't want to put myself at any more risk."

"Well, P! We just got to practice safe sex."

"Yeah, I guess we do." I said walking around him to retrieve the other ingredients for the meal.

"Here, put the onions and bell peppers in the meat." He said as he turned back around as though I had just ruined the mood.

"Derrick, I'm sorry if I made you feel a certain way. I just had a flashback of the doctor saying you are HIV positive."

"It's ok Passion. You said be patient with you. So, that's just what I'm going to do if, that will help our marriage."

I really appreciated Derrick's understanding. I couldn't wait to see what else would happen just by us cooking together. Amazingly, we ended up singing, playing, and embracing each other until we finished. In his feelings, Derrick felt the need to set the table elegantly. He lit candles, put wine on the table, and even used some of our China dishes. Therefore, he made me want to make the dinner plates match. I decorated the plates by adding a little food decoration. And to top it all. He pulled out my chair and poured the wine along with giving me a kiss on the cheek. Feeling like a queen. I sat down gracefully. Derrick was treating me the way he treated me when, we first started dating. It's just funny that, it has taken all the negativity of the past few days to get us to this point. He fed me and I fed him. After enjoying our meal. We cleaned up the kitchen together. If you were standing on the outside of our home looking in. You would have sworn we were the perfect couple with no issues.

"Do you care to join me for a bubble bath now?" I asked Derrick.

"Damn! You know I will, but I got to ask. Am I dreaming or something?" We both laughed.

"I don't know. You might be!" I said jokingly. "I'm going to the bedroom and prepare the bath. Join me when you are ready."

I proceeded to our master bathroom to prepare our bath. I lit the candles around the hot tub to continue the romantic vibe that was lingering from our dinner. Therefore, to enhance the bath. I poured bubble bath solution in the water and sprinkled bath bead of lavender scent. I even put on some romantic music. The only thing left to do was, to get in my birthday suit and wait on Derrick's grand entrance. I got in the water and began to relax. Then, I noticed Derrick entering the bathroom. I could see his mind was shadowing mine because he was already in his birthday suit. He walked over and joined me in the water. I moved forward for him to be able to get comfortably behind me. Once we were comfortable. Derrick turned on the jet system to relax and massage our bodies more. I scooted backwards pressing my backside into Derrick's manhood. Derrick began rubbing my arms with bubbles as the music played. The song by The Deele titled, Two Occasions, played softly setting the atmosphere for Derrick to sing along. I had forgotten that he could carry a tune to be a man. As he sung the lyrics, my body became more in tune with his. He vigorously kissed my neck, causing different body parts to respond. Then his hands moved from my arms unto my breast. He massaged my nipples causing more arousal between my legs, as well as between his. I proceeded to entertain his singing by massaging his body, and by placing my vagina onto his penis. At this point, I wasn't even thinking about Derrick having HIV. I stroked his manhood repeatedly, causing him to call my name, and hold me tighter. We both were engaging in the art of making love, without thinking of the past few days. I obliged him, and in return he did the same, until we both reached our climaxes.

"Passion, I love you!" Derrick moaned softly.

At this point, I believed just that. That Derrick really loved me. What we had just shared, made me feel loved. And I liked the fact that at that moment, I seemed to be all he desired. Being in his arms again, sure did feel good. So, why ruin it by thinking about the past few days. At that very moment, being trapped in the art of making love might assist in restoring our marriage.

CHAPTER

3

Lying next to Derrick all night after making love sure did feel strange. Because unfortunately, when I no longer care about things, situations, or people. I am usually finished with the relationships. I don't care to talk, be in one's presence, or think you're worthy of any of my thoughts. People often mistake my feelings for me being angry for a moment as a temper tantrum. But, for my defense. My anger has become embedded inside of me. I really want to be finished with this marriage. I just cannot let go of the anger of betrayal from Derrick and Tay. As much as I would like too. I just can't.

As time rolled on and we continue to see the doctor for checkups. Things just seemed unreal. What a curve ball life had thrown us. Leaving me with feelings of death. I felt like I would have been better off in Tay's position. Meaning, I wish I were dead. Moving on from this marriage is going to be extremely hard. Because, one day we are loving on each other and the next day we are fighting. Experiencing this, I can't help but remember the conversation my mother and I had before she passed away. I had called her to vent about Derrick's cheating behaviors.

"Hello, Passion! How are you doing?"

"Hi Momma! I'm ok, but I could be better. How are you doing?" I asked.

"Well, I guess I can say the same. But what's wrong? I can hear it in your voice." She asked.

"Momma, I just want to leave here and never come back. I have caught Derrick cheating with another woman. I don't know what I'm doing wrong that makes him want to cheat on me! I just want to be finish with this whole marriage, Mom. I'm getting to a point where I no longer care about him, but I keep accepting his lies."

"Passion, only you know when you have had enough. I can't tell you to walk out of your marriage. But what I can tell you is, Derrick's cheating is not your fault. Some men just have desires and when they don't feel like they are getting them at home. They will go outside of the home. And yes, baby you still care. You are just hurting. Look in the mirror of you and Derrick's relationship. See if you are willing to keep working at it and stop blaming yourself. Or look in that mirror and see where you are in the relationship. Are you always working alone or as a team? Then, decide if you are finished. Baby, if you want Derrick. Then fight for your marriage. Momma wants you to remember Philippians 3:12-16 that states, Not that I have already obtained this or am already perfect, but I press on to make it my own, because Christ Jesus has made me his own. Brothers, I do not consider that I have made it my own. But one thing I do: forgetting what lies behind and straining forward to what lies ahead, I press on toward the goal for the prize of the upward call of God in Christ Jesus. Let those of us who are mature think this way, and if in anything you think otherwise, God will reveal that also to you. Only let us hold true to what we have attained." My mother said with great passion.

"Thank you, Momma. So much! You always know how to make me feel better." I thanked her gracefully.

Just before we were getting ready to disconnect the call my mother said, "Oh, Passion! Baby, remember. It takes too much out of you to try and care for someone who really does not care for themselves. They also may have finished with you a long time ago, but still need you around for selfish reasons. So, they will pretend they care just too still have what they want. I love you both. But baby, think about yourself for once."

As we said goodbye. I never would have imagined that would be the last conversation I would have with my mother. She gave me great advice. If it wasn't for that conversation, I would have left my marriage a long time ago.

"Passion, wake up babe!" Derrick said shaking on my body.

"Huh?" I asked while rolling over.

"You were making noises in your sleep. Are you ok? Did you have a bad dream?" Derrick asked.

"I wouldn't say bad dream. It was more like back down memory lane with my mother."

"Oh, Ok. So, are you going into work today?" He asked.

"I guess I will. It may take some of the past few days off my mind."

"I was just thinking the same thing."

We both proceeded to get out of bed and prepare for the day. Going into work wasn't a bad idea. It would give me an opportunity to investigate some things a little more. Being a paralegal gave me certain skills that could help me get some of the answers I've been wondering about. While in college, Stephanie helped me land an internship at the Willis and Davis Law Firm and after I graduated, they offered me a position. On the other hand, Derrick and Marlon owned their own construction company. They started it after making the decision to leave the street life of selling drugs. Derrick would often say, they are now using their skills the correct way to build a successful legal business. Therefore, he could make the choice to go to work or not. But on the other hand, I needed to check in with my boss. I'm pretty sure by now, they are wondering about me and when I will return to work. I notified my boss when everything happened in case, I needed a lawyer. So, I guess it's time for me to face him and provide him with more details on what happen. This way he can provide me with insight on the whole situation.

"Derrick, I'm about to leave. Is there anything you need before I go?"

"No, Passion. Just have a good day. I think I'm going to stay around the house today and get myself together. Do you need me to do anything for you today?" He asked.

"No not really. Unless you feel like cooking dinner for me today!" I chuckled.

Derrick laughed and said, "I just might."

I opened the door to the garage and proceeded to get in the car. While backing out, I couldn't help but notice Derrick standing in the garage watching me leave. I would like to think he was just making sure I got off safely, but my woman's intuition was telling me otherwise. Was he really concerned about my safety? Or was he watching me leave so he could do what he really wanted to. At this point, it really didn't matter. Because my focus was on getting to work and what my day would hold. Therefore, I continued my daily route to work. One of my morning rituals was, to listen to gospel music in order to clear my mind of all negativities. On this morning, I noticed I needed to get some gas. Therefore, I stopped at my favorite gas station that carried the best expresso coffee and they made awesome strawberry donuts. After purchasing the items. I returned to my car and started pumping my gas. Unexpectedly, Marlon's car pulled into the gas station. As I watched him pulling in, my heart began to beat faster and faster. I wasn't sure if it was because I was excited to be in his presence. Or my excitement was related to what could transpire from a conversation. Marlon pulled right behind my car. He got out of his car and walked toward me. Staring at him strolling toward me like a black stallion. My eyes fixated on his body structure and the way he walked. He made me think of the night we made love. Once he arrived in my presence. I was also captivated by the smell of his cologne.

"Good Morning, Passion. How are you today?" Marlon asked.

"Morning, Marlon. I'm actually doing ok. How about yourself?"

"I'm well. So where are you headed right now? We really need to talk."

"I'm going into work today, but if we need to talk. I can go in later or we can meet on my lunch break."

"Ok, let's meet for lunch, that works better for me. Just call me when you are ready." Marlon said in a deep voice staring into my eyes.

"Alright, I will give you a call around 12 o'clock." I said staring back at him. The demeanor Marlon was giving off was if he was upset with me for some reason. I was wondering if, we didn't need to have the talk at that moment.

"Cool!" Marlon said as he kissed me on my lips and walked away.

I finished pumping my gas as I watched him walk in the store. I got into my car and started to wonder what Marlon wanted to talk about. The way Marlon was acting. It just didn't seem like it would be nothing positive. Pulling into traffic, I was still pondering about not going into work. Unfortunately, I drove on into work.

After arriving at work and greeting everyone with a big smile. My boss called me straight into his office.

"Hello, Passion! How are you feeling today?" Mr. Davis asked.

"Hello, Mr. Davis! I'm doing ok. Just hurt in my heart and soul."

"Are you sure coming in was a good idea so soon?"

"Yes Sir! I needed to get out of the house and away from things for a couple of hours. What better way than to come to do what I love to do."

"Ok Passion. I just wanted to let you know we are here for you and if you need anything, just let us know. And please, don't be rushing back to work for us. We are going to be fine if you need some more time off." He said with great honor.

"Mr. Davis, I really appreciate it. I will let you know if it's too much for me. I do want to let you know that I'm going to just work up until lunch today and then I'm going to leave. I want to make sure I'm not overdoing it too soon. I'm pretty sure some of my coworkers will eventually start asking questions, that I'm just not ready to answer yet."

"They shouldn't be asking any questions. We had a meeting and informed them of your privacy. Let me know if this becomes a problem!" Mr. Davis stated.

"Yes Sir. I will." I answered as I started to get up to leave the office.

Mr. Davis escorted me to the door and watched me as I walked to my office. I could tell he had a lot more to say but decided that this was not the right time. After opening my office door. I looked around the room and experienced the peace that surpassed my own understanding of things. I sat down at my desk and immediately logged into my computer. I wanted to check my emails and go over some of the cases I was working on previously. But unfortunately, as I strolled down my emails there was a particular email that stood out from the rest. It was received as being of high importance. Therefore, I immediately opened it up. As I began to read it. My heart began to feel the very pain that flooded from it back at the hotel. The email came from an unknown email address and it read:

Dear Passion,

I couldn't reach out to you any other way that I felt secure enough to do so. Therefore, I'm notifying you via your work email. Which, I found on your employer's website. I believe there is some other things you need to know about that husband of yours. I hope you didn't think your best friend was his only mistress. And I'm not talking about his high school sweetheart Candice either. I think you may need to watch an associate of yours. See I'm a friend of a friend of another friend. Who apparently know more than you? Isn't Stephanie Marlon's wife? I know you're probably wondering by now. Why have I decided to share this now? Well, why not now. Seems like you are going to need a little more ammunition to help you get clear from any actions that happen at the hotel. See, I too have been a victim of destructing friendships in which I believed were true. That's a whole other email in it itself though. I know you're wanting to hear more by now. So here it goes. You received a call that day to go to the hotel, right? Well, you should have gotten there a little earlier and you could have saw the argument between your bestie and Stephanie. See, apparently Derrick was supposed to meet Stephanie and when he didn't. She tracked him to the hotel, only to discover him and your friend entering their room. With great animosity, she got out the car and confronted him. They all went round and round with harsh words to each other. This led Derrick to make your friend go into the room to keep any physical altercations from happening. He closed the door behind her and proceeded to argue with Stephanie until she gave up and left. If you review the attachments of this email. You will see pictures of what I'm talking about. Now, I'm not the one to gossip, but it sure looked like more than anger coming from just a best friend's wife. (Laughed) It looked more like anger from another girl toy. Hum mm! Girl, you better open your eyes before you be behind bars for something you know you didn't commit. Derrick is a dog and always have been. I'm just glad I can be of service and provide this information to you. Well, I'm going to end this email for now. Don't' be alarmed if more emails arrive. Oh! There is no need to try and find out who I am. You will find out in due time. I wish you the best outcome in all of this.

Toodaloos!!!

Sincerely,
Your Secret Advisor

"After reading this email. The anger I had tried to forget in the past days, rose again. Could this be why Marlon wanted to meet? And if it wasn't. Should I even bring it up? I'm so damn confused and mad right now. I don't know if I should scream or turn my desk over. All I could hear was a small voice saying, "Calm down! I got you!" I immediately got up and locked my office door. I didn't want anyone to come in why I sobbed like a baby. Just when I wanted to believe I could move on in my marriage. Now, I'm back to square one wanting to hurt the man I said, I love so much. But to really top it off. Stephanie is just down the hallway. If she is even at work today. My hurt is telling me to go confront her, but my mind is telling me to sit back and be patient for it all to come out. How could she see me daily knowing she is sleeping with my husband? Better yet, how can she be married to Marlon knowing she is sleeping with his best friend?

"Really, Passion!" My intuition spoke and said to me. "That's just like the pot calling the kettle black when they know they both are doing the same thing!"

Maybe Mr. Davis was correct. I shouldn't have returned back to work so early. Because if I wouldn't have come in and read the emails. My feelings would have been spared a little longer.

"Knock! Knock!"

The knock on the door startled me. I looked at the door as if it were going to open after the knock. I had forgot that I had locked it earlier.

"Just one moment!" I stated as I got up and opened the door.

"Hello Passion. I am glad to see you back." Stephanie said.

"Hello Stephanie! Thanks, but I'm not sure if I'm so glad right now!" I said sarcastically.

"Well, is there something I can help with that can ease your mind?" she asked.

"No, Stephanie. I will be ok. Is there something you needed? Or is there another reason you came down?"

"No Passion. I just came to speak and check on you. I told Marlon that I wanted to give you time to recover before I bothered you. After I saw you walk in today, I decided to come and check on you."

"Stephanie, thanks so much. I wanted to come in to get a little breathing room from everything else. But I think I'm going to go ahead and go back home. Coming in today may have been a bad idea after all."

"Ok. Well call me if you need anything. I know we all need to sit down soon and talk about this situation. Marlon has been filling me in on some things and I know how you feel as a woman. I would love to be a support to you. We have been through a lot together with these two men of ours. I'll call you later to check on you." Stephanie said as she moved closer to the door.

"Thanks!" I responded. But in my mind. I really wanted to inquire about the information I had just read in the email. It was so hard not to blurt out the questions that dinged in my head while she spoke. I dare this bitch come into my office and offer support when she has been one of Derrick's side chicks. Oh yeah! We shall talk later about the situation, but will she be ready to hear what I know, and will she be accepting of the actions I have done to her as well? Right now, I really do not care. All I want her to do is get out of my office.

Just as Stephanie was closing the door my cell phone rung.

"Passion, are you available to leave now?" Marlon asked.

"Yes Marlon! I need to get out of here. Some more shit just came to me as I got here! Where do you want to meet?"

"Do you remember the place called the Junction just right outside of the city?" He asked.

"Yes, I do!"

"Meet me there. I will reserve the private room in the back, so we can have privacy."

"Ok, see you soon!"

"Alright Passion!" Marlon said strongly as if he had a lot on his mind.

I logged out of my computer and phoned Mr. Davis to let him know I was going to go ahead and leave for the day. After giving me his I told you so speech. He advised me to take some time off to get myself together. If they needed something at the office from me, he would call me. I hurriedly straightened my office back up and walked swiftly to reach the elevator to leave the building. I was so glad no one was at the receptionist desk or in the hallway. My escape to leave was a straight shot. I got in my car and headed straight for the Junction. While driving I could not help but wonder if I should share the information I had read in the email or just leave it alone for right now. But after turning on the radio and hearing the song, Stay Together by Ledisi. I might just spill the beans. Because after reading the email, will we all stay together with the one we claim we love and married. Or will we go our separate ways.

CHAPTER

4

After arriving at The Junction. I noticed Marlon's black Jaguar parked right in front of the door. So, I decided to park a way down from him, just in case someone would pass by and notice our cars. I walked to the door entrance and was brought to a halt. Looking at the outside of the building, one would never imagine that there would be security at the entrance. The outside was old in statue with wood shingles. Its outside appearance sure didn't match the inside décor. But who am I to judge?

"Hello Ma'am. How are you today? Welcome to The Junction! May I please see your driver's license or some form of ID." The security officer asked.

"Hi! Yes, you can. And I am doing better than expected. Thanks for asking." I advised.

The security officer took my ID and scanned it through a machine. The light flashed green, and he gave it back to me with a big smile on his face.

"Mrs. Wilson, are you meeting someone today, or will you be dining alone?" He asked.

"Yes, I am meeting someone. I believe he is already inside. The gentleman's name is Marlon."

The security officer looked at me in disbelief as though he knew Marlon very well.

"Yes Ma'am. Marlon is here. I am so sorry. He did not provide a name of his guest, but he did advise he was expecting a visitor." He spoke as we walked inward of the restaurant.

As he walked farther inside. I followed him looking around. I noticed that the restaurant was empty and very dark. There were people behind the bar working and a DJ on a stage for entertainment. What I thought was a restaurant seemed to be some sort of night club or strip joint. The stage intruded outward with lights around it and there were table and chairs surrounding it also. After seeing the inside, I can see why the security measures are in place.

After arriving to the private room Marlon had spoken of earlier. The security officer opened the door and informed Marlon I had arrived.

"Ok, let her in!" Marlon stated. "Come on in Passion!"

"Hey Marlon! From the looks of it you are well known around here." I said jokingly.

"You got jokes today I see!" Marlon said as he laughed.

"Yes, I need a little humor after the morning I have had."

"Well, come sit right here and tell me about it." Marlon said.

Walking over to the little sofa Marlon was sitting on. I took a seat right next to him. After sitting down, I began to look around the room. There was an office desk with a chair in one corner and a bookshelf to the left of it. Derrick and I were seated in an area that appeared to be a little living room. There was a TV mounted on the wall to review security footages of the inside and outside of the building. I also noticed a door on the right of me that appeared to be the entrance to a bathroom. I could not help but wonder whose office this may be, and why would Marlon have access to it. Therefore, I asked.

"Marlon, whose office is this?"

"Passion, you're worried about the wrong thing right now. Tell me why your morning turned out to be a bad idea. When I saw you at the gas station you were excited about going into work. What happened to ruin that?" He asked. Marlon's demeanor startled me. He has always been an incredibly soft spoking person, but for some reason today. He has this macho demeanor.

"Well! I guess it is not my business. But you cannot fault me for asking. Never mind about what happened at work. Why did you want us to meet?"

"Passion don't take my response personally. Knowing whose office this is will only open a question-and-answer section, in which I am not sure you're ready for all of that just yet. So let us just discuss why I wanted to meet in the first place."

"Ok, so why did you want to talk?"

"Derrick and I spoke about the results of his HIV testing. It left me with my mouth wide opened. I thought about us being intimate and what that meant for me. I got scared at first, but then he said you were negative. So, I wanted to see where you're state of mind is. Well, how are you dealing with the results?"

"Marlon, I am ok for now, but I am still fearful. Who's to say that my results won't change down the line. I keep getting angry at him about his cheating. But to be honest, I really can't be angry. I'm no better than he is. I slept with you. And you're his best friend."

What I said to Marlon was not what I really wanted to say to him. I wanted to say to him, you need to ask your wife how she feels. Ask her where her head is. But for now, I'm going to give limited information. To be truthful, I don't know who to trust or who is true in all these relationships. Because we all seem to be playing with each other's marriages.

"So, Passion. I see you are having regrets about what we share. Therefore, let me help you out a little bit. Do you remember all the times I called and checked up on you when Derrick was out of town on business?"

"Yes, but what does that have to do with the feelings I'm having?"

"Passion, I knew what he was doing and who he was doing it with. I would check on you to see if you really knew what he was doing and where he was going. I always felt sorry for you. He didn't realize what he had at home. You just don't know how I wished my wife was half the woman you are. She doesn't cook. I bet not ask her to clean nothing. She complains about sex and spends more money than she makes. Everything is always about her and her family. I asked her the other day about having another child. She had the nerve to come home the next day with a doll and say, here is your child. Derrick just doesn't know!" Marlon stated shaking his head.

After hearing him say this, I wanted to tell him so badly about the email. But because, I don't know if the information is the truth. I am not going to share. I kept looking at Marlon because I am confused. I have always thought of Stephanie as the model wife. Until today, after reading the email. I continued to listen to Marlon without saying a word, hoping he would say more that would relate to the information I received in the email.

"Stephanie thinks I'm stupid Passion. But I just pray that the day never comes that I run up on her, and I discover what she is doing. I can't tell you what I might do!" He said angrily.

"Marlon, what is she doing? Or what do you think she is doing?" I asked.

"Come on Passion! You can't be that dumb. She is cheating!"

"How do you know Marlon? Are you thinking this because she doesn't cook, clean, or because of the sex issues?"

"Nawl, Passion. I know this because I hired a private investigator to follow her two years ago. He brought me back information and I saw it for myself. I've been letting her slide. But after what happen to Derrick and your friend. I don't think I want to be in that situation like you. I don't want to see my best friend dead and I'm left dealing with a cheating mate. That's got to be a fucked-up feeling for you!" Marlon said as tears began to roll down his face.

Marlon had just confirmed what the email was all about. He knew Derrick and Stephanie were cheating together. He had been carrying this around for two years and never said a word. Now, I'm even more confused. Could Marlon also be the one who went to the hotel that day? Looking in his eyes right now. He could have wanted Derrick dead too. But most of all, was Marlon's feelings for me real, or were they to get back at Derrick and Stephanie? There was only one way to find out, and I jumped on the opportunity.

"Marlon. Are you saying Derrick and Stephanie are messing around?"

"Yes Passion!" He spoke.

"So, you knew this for two years and you just kept quiet. You have been hanging with him and acting as if nothing is going on. How can you? I get so nervous around the both of you. Especially knowing, I have been sexual with you. You are stronger than I could ever be."

"Passion I know you remember your mother telling you to keep your enemies closer. That's exactly what I have been doing, until I get ready to make my move."

"And what does that move consist of if I can ask?"

"A divorce!" Marlon stated.

"Well since you have spilled your beans. I guess I should too. Today when I got into my emails. Someone had sent me an email telling me about Stephanie and Derrick. They advised that they wanted to open my eyes. They didn't give a lot of information, but it was enough for me. I guess they were right. I am the only one that's in the dark about it. So, is this why you made your move on me?"

"No Passion. You didn't hear what I said before! I wished I had a woman like you. I love everything about you. The intimacy was all I hadn't shared with you. After that, I fell more in love with you. We had already been having long conversations, going out together, and sharing all kinds of stuff. On occasions, I've even been more like a husband to you than he has. Derrick thought he was being slick. He wanted me to check on you and to do this and that for him. He never imagined; I was peeping his game the whole time. Derrick was doing my wife secretly and wanted me to be so busy that I wouldn't notice it. But the jokes on him. I did as he requested. And in return it caused me to fall in love with his wife."

"Marlon, you're in love with me?"

"Yes! Imagine that. It is sad to say, but I wish it were his ass that was dead and not Tay." Marlon said sarcastically.

We continued conversations about different things, not even noticing that the time had passed 3pm. It wasn't until we received a knock at the door that we noticed the time.

"Yeah, who is it?" Marlon yelled out.

"Hey Man, It's me!" The voice on the other side of the door yelled back.

"Oh, ok. Come on in!" Marlon answered.

The door swung open and to my surprise stood a tall handsome white male. He had a crew cut hairstyle with a much-outlined salt and pepper beard along his face. This man was well built and dressed in a professional manner. He walked in and proceeded over to the desk in the corner and sat down.

"I'm sorry to intrude on you all. I needed to get something out of the desk. I will only be a quick minute." The man stated.

"Awe no problem. We are fixing to leave out. Thanks for allowing me to use the office." Marlon said.

We got up and proceeded to the door. While walking to leave the room. I couldn't help but look over at the gentleman. Only to discover, he was looking at us as we left the room too. It looks like he is as curious about me as I am of him and Marlon's relationship. They must know each other personally, because there are not too many people who will allow you to use their offices for personal use. Unless they know you.

As we walked through the restaurant, I noticed that a few people had arrived. I was sure glad that the lights were on now. It made it easier to walk through the restaurant without stumbling over anything. This way everyone was visible, and no familiar faces would go unnoticed. I sure would hate for someone to run back and tell Derrick they saw me there before I had a chance to. The restaurant was also filled with soft music playing and I could smell the aromas of different foods cooking. As far as I could see, we made it back to the security desk without being noticed. Marlon and I stepped outside to say our goodbyes. Before I could walk away. Marlon embraced me strongly and whispered a statement in my ear.

"Please be careful. And I need for you to remember everything about our conversation today. Trust me! You will thank me later." Marlon proclaimed.

I wasn't sure about what he meant. Therefore, I just nodded my head to let him know, I understood what he had just spoken. I turned and walked away in a state of uncertainty of what his statement really meant. But for some reason, inside my mind, I knew I would soon find out. After getting in my car, I noticed I had a miss call from Derrick. So, before I drove off. I wanted to call him back just in case, I needed to prepare myself for anything else.

"Hello, did you call me?" I asked.

"Yes, what time are you coming home?" Derrick asked.

"I'm actually in route now. Is there anything I need to get for you?"

Derrick said, "I was just fixing to ask you the same thing."

"No, I'm good! Are you at home or out and about?"

"I'm actually out as well. I was going to pick up dinner unless you have other plans for us."

"No, can you pick up something? If you don't mind."

"Babe, I don't. I been wanting to try the new spot Marlon has been talking about right outside of town. He told me that the food is wonderful. And today just seems like a good day to try something new. Once I get there and look at a menu. I will call you and tell you what they have." Derrick stated.

"Ok, sounds great. That will be fine. See you when you get home."

After hearing Derrick say, Marlon told him about a new restaurant right outside of town. I decided to hurry up and drive away. I even went in the opposite direction in which I believe Derrick would be traveling to get there. But the real question is, when did Marlon tell Derrick about the restaurant, and why was today the day he decided to try it out? Was Marlon trying to set me up by telling Derrick to come there today? I can smell a trap being setup, and I'm sure hoping the trapper isn't Marlon. Thinking back, Marlon did advise me to remember the conversations about today. Was that his way of giving me a clue of what may happen? Now, I'm wondering should I go back, or give Derrick a call to make sure he is ok. No, I need to just get home to make sure I'm ok. I'm pretty sure Derrick can take care of himself. He has been doing it for years just fine without me. I couldn't help but think about all of his mishaps and what he has done to me in the past. My nerves began to get the best of me again. Just like the day I drove to the hotel after receiving the call from an anonymous caller. Now getting home meant more to me than getting away from it earlier this morning. I drove home rapidly making a forty-minute drive turn into a twenty-minute drive. With gladness, I pulled into the garage and went inside. Upon getting inside, I removed my shoes and sat down at the kitchen table to get some relief.

CHAPTER

5

As I sat thanking God for allowing me to make it home safely. I began to think more about what Marlon had stated before we left the restaurant. What did he mean about remember our conversation today? Just as I started to rethink about the conversation we shared. The phone rang.

"Hello Derrick. Have you made it to the restaurant?" I said while looking at his number on the caller ID.

"Yes Passion. That's why I'm calling you. I have reviewed the menu and decided that I want a steak with a bake potato and salad. Would you like the same?" Derrick asked.

"Yes, that will be fine. You already know I would like my steak well done."

"Ok, I got it. Would you like anything else?" He asked.

"No, that's actually too much because I am really not that hungry."

"Is there anything wrong?"

"No, just a little tired and ready to relax." I explained.

"Ok Passion. Well, take you a hot bath and by the time you finish. I should be home or almost there. It might be a little longer than I expected. When I pulled in and noticed Marlon getting in his car. I stopped him, and now he is sitting here with me while I wait. I just wanted to make sure you got home safe and to see what you wanted for dinner. So, go ahead and do what you need to do. I will be home shortly babe." Derrick said eagerly.

"Ok Derrick. Tell Marlon I said hello and I will see you when you get here."

"Ok, got you!" He said as he disconnected the call.

I hung up the call and walked down the hall to enter the bedroom. As I looked around the room. I noticed that some of the dresser drawers were pulled out. I wonder what Derrick was looking for. Whatever he was looking for must have been important because the clothing inside the drawers were moved around. He knows I am a neat freak and like our clothing to remain neatly in the appropriate drawers. So, for the life of me, I can't see why he has disarranged the clothing in the drawers that they were originally placed in. Damn, why would he leave such a mess? Continuously looking around the room. I started picking up clothing and placing them back where they went. But as I bent down to pick up this one shirt. I sat on the floor staring at the words that were wrote across the front. The word stated, "Friends 4Ever." This was a t-shirt Tay and I had made regarding our bond as friends. Now that I sit looking at it. I started to think about her being gone. Selfishly, I became sad and began to cry. I was not sure if my tears were a sign of gladness or sadness. How could someone who stated they were my friend do what she had done. But I will never be able to ask her why. All I must hold onto about someone I called my friend, and even my sister is that she was cheating with my husband! I could not help but scream.

"Why Tay! Why! What did I do so badly to you?"

I started to rip the shirt apart with my bare hands. With every rip came a different tear. And with every different tear came anger that rapidly built into a mighty scream. This whore stabbed me in my back the whole time, while smiling in my face. I can only imagine how she must have thought highly of herself. See, Tayneshia was the one who gloated in getting what she wanted by any means necessary. It didn't matter to her who she hurt, just as long as she felt good. Well, I wish I could see how highly she thinks about herself now. Could she gloat about her desires causing her death? I don't think so. Looks like I am the rabbit with the gun now.

I got up from on the floor and went outside in the backyard. I found the old can Derrick used to dump his marijuana ashes in and put the ripped t-shirt pieces in it. I threw a match in the can and watched the shirt burn down. This gave me a sense of relief. Derrick had advised me to take a hot bath for some relaxation, but this gave me much more. This made me get a piece of revenge. Because this shirt once meant the world to me. Now it means the world to me to get rid of it. I can honestly say I know how Bernadette felt in the Waiting to Exhale movie, right after she burned her husband's clothes in his car. Her revenge for him cheating with a white woman was to burn what cost him a lot. I even strutted back into the house just like she did. The only thing is, I didn't have a cigarette in my hand to esteem me more. Just as I got inside the house, I heard the back door open and in came Derrick.

"Passion, why are you looking at me like that?" Derrick asked.

"Because I want to know what you were looking for in the dresser drawers. You left such a mess." I said angrily.

"Oh, I was looking for the arm support I wear when I go exercise. My arm was throbbing a little. I thought if I wore it. It would help with the aching. I'm sorry. I will straighten it all back up." He explained like a kid getting scolded by their parent.

"Too Late! I already straightened the drawers back up."

"Passion, what is it? I know that is not why you look so angry." Derrick stated.

"No, I found a shirt that bought back old memories of Tay. So, I wanted it gone. Therefore, I went out back and burned it in your marijuana can. I was coming back inside the same time you were walking in."

Derrick shucked his head and said jokingly, "I dare not ask any more questions about that. I know when to leave well enough alone."

"I'm so glad you do!" I stated with a straight face as I looked at him.

I wanted him to say the wrong thing in order to give me the chance to explode more about the situation. But Derrick was no fool. He kept on getting the dinner out the bags and placing it on the table. He was refusing to get into my anger space and become the next target. As he finished getting everything together.

He looked at me and said, "Let's eat! Do you want me to say grace, or would you like to?"

"No, you can. I wouldn't dare talk to God with this attitude." We both laughed as Derrick prepared to lead us in prayer.

"Our Father in Heaven, we give thanks for the pleasure of being together as husband and wife again.

We also give thanks for this food prepared before us.

As we partake of this food, we pray for health and strength to carry on.

Lord, please don't allow the anger Passion has right now to ruin our dinner time.

This we ask in the name of Christ, Our Heavenly Father. Amen."

I looked at Derrick as though I wanted to use the knife for some other reason besides to cut my steak. His prayer was a little sarcastic for me. Therefore, I continued to stare at him wanting him to stare back at me. But Derrick never acknowledged my stare. He just accepted the look and carried on eating his dinner. After the sarcastic prayer, we really didn't say much. We just enjoyed the meal that was before us in silence.

"How did you like the food Passion?" Derrick asked.

"It was actually good. The steak was tender, and the potato was on point. I could definitely eat there again."

"Me too. So, what's up for the evening?"

"I just want to relax and go to sleep. The day has been a very trying day. Going to work wasn't as such a good idea as I thought. I found out more shit to pile on the other shit, that was already stinking in our lives."

"What are you talking about? Did someone say something about the shooting to you at work? You should have known people would be ready to question you to get information." Derrick stated.

"No one asked me any questions. It was an email I received that has me in an uproar. And I dare you try to tell me I should have knew this and that! What I should have known was that my husband was sleeping with my best friend and other women."

"Passion, what are you talking about other women for? I thought we had this talk the other night and decided we were going to move forward in life. We can't move forward in this marriage if you are going to keep bringing shit up. You and I both know people are going to try and put their two cents on what happen. We can't give them that privilege. Well, I know I'm not going to give it to them." He proclaimed.

"That's easier for you to say! You're not the one looking like a big dummy and a fool. Derrick, this hurts! I'm trying to smile and move on, but when little trinkets of different information keep getting dropped on me. It's hard to forget, forgive, and move on. I need you to really be honest, and just spill the milk about everything and every woman. I just don't know how much more I can take. Especially, when people know things that I don't, and now they feel the need to share what they know. I wish you could really put yourself in my shoes."

"Passion, I recall you telling me years ago not to cry over spilled milk. It was your words that said once milk is spilled you can't retrieve it. The only thing you can do is soak it up by any means necessary. So why are you continuing to cry over things we cannot do anything about now. You also said really to soak the milk up, you must learn a lesson from it, and move on. So, you mean to tell me you can't accept your own advice? Because it looks like that to me, you are trying to retrieve some of the spill milk again. You also said to me when milk is spilled, things get into it and it's not worth having any longer. So, are you trying to tell me this marriage is not worth having anymore, because of the trinkets someone dropped today? Passion, please do not allow the spill milk to ruin our lives. I am even going to go a little farther and recite a scripture from the bible. In Genesis 7, Noah concentrated on what God had given him to do and left the rest to God. If we are saying we want to work on this marriage like grown adults. We have got to concentrate on what God wants us to do and let him do the rest. Yes, this may mean a lot of more information may come to the forefront, but we got to soak the bad and the good up. Therefore, Passion if you want me to spill all of the milk. Let's do it! But babe, please be sure you will not panic and run away from me. I'm not sure if I can take any more heart break in my life."

"Derrick, I dare you try to use my own words on me. Because I'm not the one who spilled the milk that brought us to this point. Yes, I recited those words to you years ago. But dammit, all I want is for you to be truthful. Ok! What if the shoes were on the other foot? Your foot! Would you let it go and move on? Hell, no you would not! My head probably would be knocked off my body with the temper you can get. Derrick don't try to make this all about me not being able to soak this up. Look how many times you've spilled milk. If you don't want me crying over spill milk. You should have remembered that old saying, Love should have brought your ass home last night. Especially, all those times you desired the other women. Boy, I wish I would sit here and let you flip this all on me."

At this point, nothing Derrick said meant anything to me. I got up and pushed the chair under the table and proceeded to grab the remaining of my dinner to put away. I didn't want him to say another word right now. I may have wanted the truth, but now was just not the time. He once again had flipped the conversation and situation to make me feel bad.

The evening was winding down. And any further conversations with Derrick at this point had winded down too. Looking at the time, it really was too early to go to bed. Therefore, I decided to go to our exercising room Derrick built in the backyard. Doing exercise at this point could allow me to release some of my anger. Sad to say, but the exercising room lately had become a place I could release any frustrations without hurting another. It also allowed me to stay on a track of remaining healthy. See, after some of life's events that happened to me. It has been extremely hard for me to balance my weight. It constantly fluctuates up and down. For many years, I believed this was why Derrick constantly cheated on me. Because when I thought about the women he cheated with. They all have nice physiques. He even reiterated sometimes that he preferred women with a coke bottle shape. And at times I was far from that statue. So, I try and work on my own physique to keep a form of body acceptability for him. I even hoped it would cause him to desire me and not them. But the world could see that didn't work.

Entering the exercising room. I turned on the lights and put in some music to motivate myself. Usually, when I exercise. I loved to listen to rap music. But today for some reason, I had the urge to listen to some R&B music. As I climbed on the treadmill, all I could hear playing in the background was Keith Sweats' song, Make it Last Forever. It was playing on the play list and his voice appeared to resemble the voice of Derrick screaming the lyrics of this song to me. Funny thing is, will we make it last forever now that everything is coming out? Or will my hurt and pain last forever? Currently, in the state I'm in, I really could care less about everyone else's feelings. And for sure now, I am not going to feel any guilt for my own actions. I really want to get revenge on everyone. As these feelings of revenge increased. I immediately turned up the speed on the treadmill only to experience a burning sensation in my left leg. I was so eager to get away from Derrick and relieve my anger, that I forgot to do some warmup exercises. My body started to remind me of what I didn't do before pushing it to a different level. Therefore, I stopped the treadmill and started to do some yoga exercises. I pulled out the mat and sat on the floor to meditate. Right when my mind was getting some relief. The phone rang. I sprung myself to my feet and grabbed my phone off the treadmill.

"Hello!"

"Hello Passion! This is Janelle. I hope you are doing ok, and I pray you're ok with me calling you right now."

Janelle is Tayneshia little sister. I really was not expecting this call, and really did not care to hear what she had to say. But there are some curiosities within me, that just maybe Janelle could answer. Tayneshia and her sister were close. I'm almost certain she knew of her messing with Derrick. But I doubt if she was calling to be an informant. Therefore, I am going to listen for only a short while to what she has to say. I am trying to relieve anger, not add to it.

"Hi Janelle. How can I help you today?" I said sarcastically.

"Well, I know you know what happen to Tay, and I just wanted to check on you to make sure you are ok. Despite the circumstances, I know how much you both loved each other." She stated.

"Janelle, I do not mean to sound rude. But I don't give two fat rats about your sister after what she has done to me. Yes, I'm sorrowful for the family having to deal with her death. But technically, I'm glad she got what she deserved. And furthermore, I dare you call me acting like you're checking on me. I'm damn sure you knew about the affair. Whatever your motive is for this call. I do not know. But thanks, and no thanks!"

"Passion, I didn't know shit! But my sister is dead, no matter if she was cheating with your husband or not. You get to still have your husband, but we do not have her anymore. And you need to remember, it took two to tango. I'm sorry you feel the way you do. I'm not sure why Tay chose to cheat with your husband knowing you all were friends. But she didn't deserve to die. I'm sorry for calling you. I only called to check on you. But fuck you and your cheating ass husband!" She yelled as she hung up the phone in my face.

Now, I am sitting here sobbing ferociously. Not because Janelle said what she said. But because, I am having feelings of regret for Tay. She was correct. Their family do not get to have nothing but memories of her. Why couldn't Tay and Derrick have remained faithful to their vows? Tay had a husband and Derrick had me. I wonder how Mark is feeling now. Does he know that Tay was with Derrick at the hotel? How are her children reacting to it? All these questions raced in my head.

"Passion, did you really have to be that rude? Why didn't you hear her out more and maybe you wouldn't be having regrets? Now, we will never know the answer to our questions." My conscious stated to me.

Well, I could not change the situation now. Eagerly, I started back with my yoga hoping to drown out my conscious. Also hoping that this time, I could complete the yoga, and get back to relieving some tension on the treadmill. After finishing a much-needed workout. I decided to stay in the exercising room a little longer even though nightfall had arrived. At this point, I just wanted to relax and be my own company. Usually, after a good work out, I would prefer a nice long shower. But this time, I just wanted to remain alone. Drenched with wetness, I slung my tiresome body onto the sofa Derrick placed in the room for comfort. I continued to listen to my R&B. The music was so calming to my spirit, that I drifted swiftly into a deep sleep.

CHAPTER

6

I was awakened by the sound of thunder and I immediately jumped. After looking around the dark room, I noticed I was still in the exercising room. Funny thing is, how did my favorite blanket get thrown across me, and who turned out the lights? I began searching for my phone because, I wanted to check on what time it was. Only to find out, it was 3am in the morning. I guess I have out stayed my welcome out here. So, I decided to go inside. I bet Derrick is fast asleep. It was kind of nice of him to bring my favorite blanket and cover me up. He knows how I cherish it and hate to sleep without it. This blanket was not only warm but meant so much to me. It was giving to me when I was in the sixth grade by one of my brothers. I have kept it through the years. The blanket's appearance has remains beautiful. It doesn't have any snags, and its color is still flawless. My family and friends often refer to me as Linus off the cartoon Charlie Brown. I carry my blanket everywhere, and do not like others to use it. I often refer to the horse design, as being my rescuer in the times I need comfort. For some reason, this blanket made me feel secure. I wasn't sure if it was because my brother gave it to me. Or, because it really was a great support of comfort and warmth. And the beautification of the design and color made it even more special.

Grabbing the blanket, I decided it was time to go into the house. Upon trying to go back into the house, I noticed that it was storming badly. Therefore, I shut the door, and returned to the sofa. As I got comfortable back under my blanket, I saw a shadow flash by the window. At first, I thought it was a tree limb. But after staring. I could tell it was a shadow of a person. This startled me with fear. I quickly sprung to my feet and rush to lock the door. Unfortunately, I wasn't quick enough. The shadow I saw was grabbing the door handle, at the same time I was trying to lock it. The door flung open and standing there drenched from the rain stood Marlon.

"What are you doing here?" I asked trying to speak softly. I didn't want Derrick to hear or see Marlon.

"I come to get you. Come on now! We need to go!" Marlon stated rapidly.

"Marlon, you have got to be out of your mind! Derrick is inside. What if he sees you? Better yet, sees us leaving together. You are going to damn far Marlon. Get out of here!"

"Passion, come on here! Derrick is not even in the house. I saw him leave about two hours ago." Marlon explained.

"What are you talking about? You saw him leave. Are you stalking us now?"

"Girl, will you come on here! I will tell you more in the car."

Looking at Marlon in his eyes I could tell something was wrong. So, I grabbed his hand. He had placed his hand out for me to grab onto it. He was trying to assist me with walking through the muddy backyard to get around to his car. By the time we reached his car out front, we both were soaked. Marlon opened the passenger door and closed it. He ran around the car and got inside. He immediately turned on the heater. Then drove off in a fast speed.

"Are you going to tell me what's going on?" I asked.

"Passion, I called Derrick earlier to see how you all liked the food. He advised me that you all enjoyed it, but you were tripping because you had found out something else today. He then told me you were out back exercising, and he was thinking about going out for a drink. He went on to say, he needed some time away from you, but did not want you to be questioning him. He asked me if I wanted to accompany him at the bar for drinks. He felt if you were to ask later about him going out, you would be ok if he was with me. I explained to him it was raining and I was not going to come out in it. Derrick later called me back and said, "If Passion calls you tell her I'm with you. And if she asks for me, say I'm in the restroom or something." This let me know he was up to no good. Then after his last call to me, Stephanie started getting an attitude. Everything I did made her angry. She then shouted, "I need to get away from you for a while. I'm going to my sister's house." Now, you and I both know Stephanie doesn't like to drive in the rain. So, what makes tonight so special. This bitch even had the nerves to take an overnight bag. Passion, she really thinks I'm that stupid. See, after I discovered them cheating, I put a tracker on her car, and I can see it on my phone. So, I gave her some time and I left behind her. I didn't follow her, because I can track her. So, I came over here and sat down the road to see if Derrick was really going to leave. And guess what, he left just like I suspected."

"So how did you know I was still in the exercising room?"

"Because I rang the doorbell repeatedly and you never answered. That let me know you had to be still in there. Luckily, Derrick used the backyard gate to come around to leave. He forgot to lock it back. So, I came through it. He locked the back door as well. I checked it. He was trying to make sure you could not get into the house and see he was gone. Passion, if they are together. I'm fixing to let them have it. I'm not sparing neither one of their asses."

"Wait! Wait! Marlon. We don't' know if he went where she is at. Maybe she really went to her sister's house and he went to the bar!"

"Passion, stop with the bullshit! The tracker shows her at the Dawn Hotel on Clemson Drive." Marlon stated.

Driving erratically in the rain Marlon had me on edge. I was praying in my head that Derrick and Stephanie were not at the hotel together. I could not face another episode of what happened before. Surely, Derrick could not be this stupid to put himself in the predicament again. But I started to think just maybe he would. He constantly cheated thinking everything was always gravy. So why wouldn't he do it now. After these thoughts embraced my mind. I prayed harder and harder. Glimpses of what could happen after we arrived, traveled swiftly within my head. I had to close my eyes to focus on my silent prayer. In doing this, tears flowed down my cheeks. I finally opened my eyes and noticed we were turning into the hotel parking lot. I started shaking my legs from side to side. My nerves had started to get the best of me.

"Marlon, please think about this! You don't need to do anything crazy. Let's just park out of sight and wait!" I said nervously while putting my hand on top of his.

"Passion, I'm going to wait alright! You can stay in the car. I'm fixing to go to the clerk and see if there is a room in anyone of their names. I'm going to get the room number and knock on the damn door! I'm tired of playing with them both!" He yelled at me.

"But Marlon! We have been doing the same thing they have been doing. You and I even made love in our bed. We are no better than them. This is crazy!" I said with tears rolling from my eyes.

"So, you are going to compare what we did to what they are doing? They have been doing this mess for years. I don't care what you are saying right now Passion. Everything is going to come out in the open today. Like I said. You can wait in the car or you can come with me." Marlon stated aggressively.

Staring at me, Marlon reached under his seat and pulled out his gun.

"Marlon, why do you need that? Please, put that away! I know you are hurting, but no one needs to get hurt. The best thing is to let them see we know and just leave. What good will it do if you shoot them? Then you will have to be worried about getting into trouble and facing jail time. Trust me, they are not worth it! Okay, Okay! If you put that away. I will go with you."

With a deep sigh, Marlon placed the gun back under his seat and opened his door to get out. I was a little relieved by his action and joined him with getting out of the car. The rain had tapered off giving us one less thing to worry about. As we walked to the hotel office I looked over at Marlon. He held a straight face and walked quickly to the door. I on the other hand dreaded even going in the door. Therefore, once we got to the door. I was hesitant.

"Marlon, go on in. I will wait for you out here."

"Ok Passion! Just stand on this side of the building. I don't want them to come out and see you before we get there." He explained.

"Ok."

Marlon went on in and approached the clerk. I couldn't see or hear what he asked her, but whatever he asked. She obliged him with the information he needed because he came back out quickly.

"Passion!" He called out as he came out of the door.

"Here I am Marlon. You sure you want to do this?"

"Yes! Are you sure?" Marlon asked.

"We are here now. Let's go down there! I guess it's really time for me to face the music."

Marlon and I strolled down the sidewalk like we were authority figures going to arrest our prey. We were on a mission and there was no turning back. We wanted to arrest them for their actions without thinking about ours. While walking down the sidewalk, I begun to rehearse in my head what I wanted to say to Derrick. Would I result to physical abuse and can I take seeing him with Stephanie? Well, it was a little too late to have these thoughts. Because now the big moment had arrived. We were standing in front of the room number the clerk had provided Marlon. Looking at me, Marlon knocked on the door. At first, we heard dead silence but eventually we could hear sounds of human feet moving around. Then a lady's voice said from on the other side of the door.

"Who is it?"

Neither one of us said a word. Marlon even had placed his finger over the peak hole to make sure they couldn't see us. Then the voice yelled out louder than before.

"Who is it and what do you want? Take your damn hand off from over the peak hole, or I'm going to call the police!" The lady voice stated.

We still didn't respond, and Marlon never took his hand off from over the peak hole. I wasn't sure if Marlon was thinking like I was, but the voice that was responding did not sound like Stephanie. I couldn't figure out where I had heard the voice before, but for some reason I didn't think it was Stephanie's voice. Finally, we could hear the locks being removed from the door. As the door slowly came open. Marlon pushed me to the right side of the entrance. I guess he was protecting me from anything that may occurred after the door came open. But to our surprise what we saw after the door open startled us both, causing us to look at each other in dismay. There stood Candice a in a black negligee and Stephanie was sitting up on the side of the bed in her bra and panties. I immediately started looking around the room to see if I could spot Derrick. It didn't seem he was in that area, but who's to say if he wasn't hiding in the bathroom.

Marlon shouted out angrily, "What the fuck is going on here?"

Stephanie stood up and started grabbing her clothes from a chair nearby. She didn't say one word. She was too busy trying to get dress. But on the other hand. Candice couldn't wait to respond.

"What does it look like Marlon? We are having a girls' night out!" She said as she chuckled.

Marlon didn't find what she said funny at all. He pushed her to the side and walked toward the bathroom. I guess he was thinking like me that Derrick was hiding in the bathroom or closet area. Once he looked through to the bathroom. He immediately turned around and came back out.

He said, "So it's just you two in here?"

"Were you all looking for someone else? Humm, maybe Derrick!" Candice said sarcastically as she turned and looked at me. "No Marlon! It's just the girls tonight."

"Bitch! You've got me fucked up. I'm not Derrick or Curtis. I won't play your little games. You better learn to shut your damn mouth before I shut it for you!" Marlon said as he walked past her trying to get to Stephanie before she got out the door.

Stephanie still hadn't responded to any of Marlon's questions. She had completely gotten dressed and was trying to get out of the door before Marlon approached her. Unfortunately, her attempt was unsuccessful. Marlon grabbed her by her left arm and yanked her backwards causing her to fall in the door entrance. Just before Marlon could use his left hand to strike Stephanie. I grabbed his arm.

"Marlon!" I yelled. "Don't do that!" I pleaded.

"Passion, she deserves it! She's been playing me for a fool for years. Here I am thinking she is messing around with a man and she is in here with this nasty bitch. Stephanie, Passion has saved your ass right now. But she can't save you all the time. Slut, go get all of your shit out of my house and don't come back. Oh yeah, and don't you wake my damn daughter up either. She is going to stay with me." Marlon proclaimed as he stepped over her on the floor. "Come on Passion! Let's go! These two bitches can have each other."

Obliging Marlon's request. I turned around to walk away, but not before rolling my eyes at Candice. I wanted her to know that I saw through her little body actions and words. I grabbed Marlon's hand as we headed toward the car. I could only imagine what was running through his head now and how he was feeling. He went to try and catch his best friend and his wife together. Only to find her there with another woman. And it wasn't any better that the woman was Candice. I couldn't help but wonder. What is Candice's angle? It seems she enjoys making men and women defy their mates. I'm not sure of what her trap is for all of us. But it is sure time to find out and turn the tables back on her ass. I've just about had enough of her in my life.

CHAPTER

7

Getting in the car, I glanced over at Marlon to see if he was ok. I saw that he was staring back at the hotel room. I wasn't sure of why he was just staring and driving out of the parking lot. Therefore, I addressed him because I kept thinking of the gun that was under the seat. I didn't want him to act on the thoughts that maybe running through his head right now.

"Marlon, are you ok?" I asked. As I watched his tears quiver slowly out his eyes.

Marlon turned and looked at me and spoke.

"Passion, I know how you feel now! I knew she was cheating, but I never actually caught her in the act. I saw the pictures the investigator bought to me, but now I'm wondering if she and Derrick are really messing around. The pictures just showed her, and Derrick together, but never really showed any serious intimacy. Maybe Derrick knew of her and Candice and that's why they were meeting secretly. He was trying to inquire about their relationship. This shit is crazy and I'm not understanding it at all! Passion, I'm so sorry! I have made you come with me and Derrick wasn't even here. Damn! I really want to get back out this car and kill Candice myself. She has been the same selfish bitch since high school. P, I just don't know how these two came to hook up! Stephanie didn't go to the same high school as we did. So where did they meet and how?" Marlon stated as he finally drove out of the hotel parking lot.

"Marlon, I'm in awe myself. Because I really thought Derrick would be here too. After getting that email today. I believed it was possible. I never rule out anything when it comes to Derrick and his cheating.

"Well Passion. We can rule out the fact that he wasn't in the room just now." Marlon stated.

"Marlon, after tonight, I'm really skeptical of the email. For some reason, the way Candice was talking and looking at me back there, has me thinking she knows about that email. For now, I'm going to sit back and see if I get another one. But damn, Marlon! I would have never imagined Stephanie in this way. Where you aware that she liked women?"

"Passion, I didn't know she was into them for her own purposes. One year I was joking around with her and told her I wanted to have a threesome for my birthday. Well, that year for my birthday. I came home and to my surprise, my joke became a reality. Stephanie opened the door and escorted me to our bedroom. When I entered the room there were rose pedals on the bed, on the floor, and a trail of pedals that led to the bathroom. Candles were lit, and soft music was playing. Stephanie had on a red lace nighty with some red slippers, and her perfume reaped from her skin. Once we arrived in the bathroom. I noticed a female relaxing in a bubble bath. The female was in her birthday suit, which allowed me to see she had a banging body. She had long silk hair and appeared to be mixed with different nationalities. But what was so peculiar about her, was her eye color. They were of a light emerald-green color, and from the glare of the candlelight they sparkled more. Stephanie undressed me and all I could think about was how pretty she was. Her beauty enticed me. I couldn't help but ask Stephanie who she was. Stephanie never gave me a name. She just advised that she was my birthday gift, and she continued to undress me, until I was completely undressed. I began kissing Stephanie up and down her neck, while I removed her nighty. I continued to bring pleasure to my wife by stroking her body from top to bottom. After Stephanie and I had made each other reach a certain intimacy peak, we climbed into the bathtub with the female. I continued caressing Stephanie and the female began to caress and kiss me. Stephanie pushed me closer to the female. This surprised me. She always said, she didn't want to share me with anyone. But this night, she was ok with sharing me."

As Marlon drove and told me his story. I couldn't help but stop him during the conversation. I was so shocked at what he was saying that I wanted to make sure he didn't have any clue of who that female was. Because the description he was giving, sounded just like a female who worked with Stephanie and I at the law firm.

"Marlon, so you didn't know the female?" I asked.

"No, Passion and I still don't know who she is." He stated.

"Ok, I was just curious because you've never shared this story with me before."

"No, I haven't. I did not want you to look at me different."

"Marlon. Did you actually have intercourse with the female, or did she just caress you?"

"Passion, I did. After I saw that Stephanie was comfortable with me touching and kissing on the female. I started doing things to her as well. Stephanie even shocked me more when she whispered into the female's ear and escorted her to get on top of me. She even placed my manhood inside of the other woman. As the woman moaned and groaned while stroking me. I noticed Stephanie caressing herself. This let me know she was turned on from the intimacy the woman and I were experiencing. We continued that night doing any and everything that brought all of us pleasure. After the sexual escapades, the female left, and I've never saw her again. I asked Stephanie repeatedly afterwards who the lady was, but she would never tell me. She would just say it was not my business to know who she was. She advised me she checked her out before inviting her into our bedroom."

"So have you all ever done that again?" I questioned.

"Passion. That was our first and last time. Why did you ask that?" Marlon asked.

"Oh, no reason. I'm just trying to make sense of why Candice and Stephanie would be doing what they are doing."

"Yeah, that is a good question." Marlon said while shaking his head. "So, Passion. You and Derrick have never had a threesome?"

"No Sir! I'm just not into that sort of thing. It's bad enough that he cheats. I don't think I could stomach watching him be with another woman. And from what I've been told. When you do threesome. Either the woman or the man ends up desiring the person they invited into their bedroom. This usually causes their relationship to be destructed."

"Well, I guess that's a little true. Look at Stephanie now. She is not with the one she invited in our bedroom, but she is with a woman." He said as he turned onto my street. "Do you want me to call Derrick to see where he is?" Marlon asked.

"Yes. Since he thinks he has me locked in the exercising room and I'm fast asleep."

Marlon dialed Derrick's number and waited on him to answer. Derrick's phone wrung a long time before he finally answered.

"Hello!" Derrick whispered.

"Derrick! Where are you?" Marlon asked as he parked two houses down from ours.

"Marlon, I'm at home. Why? What's up?"

"I was just checking on you. You never called me back to let me know if you were really going out."

"Oh Shit! I went out, but I came back in about an hour ago. I just had a couple of drinks and came back home." Derrick said.

"Oh, Ok. So did Passion know you left?" Marlon asked.

"Hell no. She is still asleep in the exercising room. I'm going to let her sleep out there until in the morning. When I checked on her before I left, she was fast asleep. Therefore, I'm good. She won't even know I left out." He said positively.

"Ok Derrick. I was just checking on you. I will holler at you tomorrow. Boy, I got something to tell you!" Marlon told Derrick excitedly.

"Cool! Talk to you then." Derrick said.

Marlon hung up the phone and looked at me. We knew Derrick did not have a clue that I wasn't home. Therefore, I told Marlon to drive in the alley behind the house. There were a couple of boards that were loose in our fence, and I was going to slide through them to enter the backyard. Marlon did as I advised.

"Passion, once again. I'm sorry about tonight. I really thought they were together."

"Marlon, we still can't rule that out. Especially, now since you said you all have had a threesome. I can't help but wonder if Derrick may have been there and just left before we got there. And you know Candice is going to make sure he knows we came to the hotel together. That tramp isn't going to let us off easy. Especially, since we caught them together."

"Yeah, I guess you are right. But we shall see. Passion don't mention anything to him unless, he says something to you about it. When I talk to him tomorrow. I'm not even going to bring you up. This way we will see if he is in contact with any one of them."

Marlon leaned over and kissed me on my jaw and asked did I need helped getting through the fence. I assured him I could get through with no problem. Marlon and I hugged each other for a moment, and I proceeded to get into the backyard. My attempt to move the boards, and gain access to the backyard was a success. I splattered through the wet yard and made it back inside the exercising room. Once inside, I found a towel that we kept in the room for perspiration to wipe my shoes off. Because I was now wide awake and wanted to make sure Derrick didn't receive any kind of messages about tonight. I decided to go to the back door to see if it was still locked as Marlon stated. As I twisted the doorknob. The door came open. The house was completely dark. Derrick didn't even have the night light on that we usually burned over the stovetop. Therefore, I felt my way through the den, and then down the hallway to our bedroom. Upon arriving in the bedroom, I noticed Derrick phone was flashing. I became fearful that the flash could mean he had just received some type of notification. Could it be from Candice or Stephanie? I wasn't sure. Therefore, I turned on the light to try and draw his attention from the phone.

"Damn Passion! That light is bright babe. Hurry up and turn it off." He said frowning his face up.

"I'm sorry, but how come you left me in the exercising room all night?"

"Passion you were sleeping so good. I didn't want to bother you. So, I covered you up with your favorite blanket."

"Yeah, I did get some good sleep. Thanks." I spoke.

"What time is it?" Derrick asked.

"It's almost 7am and I'm going to take a shower. Care to join me?" I asked.

I knew I had to find a way to keep Derrick from looking at his phone. For some reason, I just knew the flashing was in relevance to what happened last night. If I could turn his attention on something different other than his phone. I might have a chance at intercepting the information before he saw it. I knew Derrick would go into the hall bathroom to get his favorite soap before he joined me in the master bathroom. He is just like a kid who always wants to play with their favorite rubber ducky in the bathtub. Derrick is so predictable. He went straight to the other bathroom. After he left the room, I ran and got his phone. Just as I suspected. There was a voicemail message from Candice. Derrick had the kind of phone that his voicemail messages would type out in a text message if missed. Therefore, I was able to see that she wanted him to call her ASAP. Unfortunately, he won't be able to do that now, because I hurriedly erased the message and put his phone back down. I was able to get back in the bathroom in time enough to start pulling my clothing off before Derrick could see me with his phone. He came in and joined me in taking a morning shower. While taking a shower I noticed the wounds Derrick received from the shooting. I began to run my hand over the gun wound while looking into Derrick's eyes.

"Does this still hurt badly?" I asked as I pressed my hand against his chest.

"It hurts, but not bad. If I turn a certain way, it throbs. "Derrick replied as he placed his hand over mine.

Derrick gripped my hand tightly with his left hand. Using his right hand, he grabbed my other hand and placed it around his neck. He leaned forward and kissed my lips. Unfortunately, I didn't reciprocate a return kiss. Because, I still had animosity from the night before. I only engaged in a shower with Derrick to keep him from seeing his phone. And plus, I am still not convinced that he may not have been at the hotel with Candice and Stephanie. The way Candice asked were we looking for Derrick instead of her let me know that she knows a lot. While thinking about Candice words. I quickly slipped my hand out of Derrick's hand. I was just being inquisitive about his wound and I didn't mean anything sexual about touching him. Therefore, I returned to washing my body. Derrick and I completed our showering and got dressed. Since it was still earlier in the morning, I suggested that we get some much-needed rest and Derrick agreed. We laid in the bed in a fetus position together. Derrick embraced me and I accepted it. He placed his arms around me and wrapped one of his legs crossed the top of mine. For some reason, I felt a great comfort that caused me to drift vastly to sleep.

CHAPTER

8

As my body found comfort, so did my mind. I could see me running through a field of different beautiful flowers. Dreaming of twirling and spinning in the flowers, made me think about how as a child my grandmother would often tell us to give others their flowers before it was too late. But unfortunately, I cannot remember anyone giving me any of life's flowers. Especially now, since I am so trapped in a marriage that repeatedly causes me devastation. Is this my reality or am I dreaming? Running farther in the field and continuing to admire the beautiful scenery, this must be a dream! Turning and twisting with the wind blowing on my face. I stumbled over a big rock. In which caused me to fall flat on my face. While on my face, I saw a picture of two eyes with droplets of tears dropping down in the dirt.

"Passion, Passion! Babe get up." Derrick yelled.

I opened my eyes to see me on the floor next to our bed.

"Wow! How did I get down here?" I stated as Derrick helped me up on the bed.

"Passion, you had to be dreaming and rolled out of the bed. I heard a bump up against the bed. That's how I woke up." Derrick stated.

"Yeah, I was dreaming of being in a field of beautiful flowers. I fell in the dream and saw crying eyes. I guess that's when I fell out of the bed. What a coincidence. I'm glad I didn't hit my head on the nightstand."

"Me too. That's what I was just thinking." Derrick said.

Looking over at the clock on the nightstand. I noticed the time stated it was after 12pm. We had slept through the rest of the morning. It was now time for us to get up and face whatever adventures today may bring. I'm pretty sure one of the adventures would be a result of what took place from last night. After getting dressed, I went into the kitchen to grab me a bowl of Special K cereal. While pouring the milk into the cereal, all I heard was a whistling sound coming toward my left ear. When I turned to see what it was. My left eye met Derrick's fist. I fell backward from the impact of the hit and fell over on the countertop. I was struggling to get my balance back when Derrick struck me again. After repeated blows to the face and head, I couldn't help but lay on the floor. Dazed from the physical abuse I had just endured. All I could do was cry and scream out, STOP Derrick!

"What the fuck were you doing with Marlon last night at a hotel? Here I am thinking you was in the exercising room sleep. But no! Your ass somehow fooled me. I want answers and I want them now!" Derrick yelled. "And you bet not lie to me!"

"Derrick, what are you talking about? I was here!"

"Passion! I just received a call from Stephanie saying she caught you and Marlon at the hotel on Clemson Drive. When she approached y'all. Marlon pushed her down and told her to get her shit and get out his house. Now, answer my damn question. What the fuck is going on? Is that the reason Marlon called me late last night trying to see if I was at home?" Derrick said angrily.

Staring at Derrick in disbelief that he had just physically assaulted me. I answered, "There is nothing going on. Yes, I was with Marlon last night, but not how it has been brought back to you."

Before I could say more. The doorbell rang. I looked at Derrick in disgust, but at the same time I was relieved. Whoever that is, didn't have a clue that they may have just saved me from more bodily harm. Derrick stepped away from me and went to answer the front door. While he was going to see who it was, I scrambled to get up because my body was racking with pain. I made it to my feet and tried to hurry to get to the bedroom. I wasn't sure of what damage Derrick had caused to my face. After getting into the room, I made it to the mirror. Looking in the mirror brought on a stream of tears. Here I stood with a busted lip and my jaw swelling quickly. Not to mention my left eye was filled with red splotches from corner to corner. I dare this asshole hit me, all because Stephanie called him. He didn't have the decency to ask me first about the situation. He used physical force to ask. I now believe what everyone is saying. Stephanie and Derrick have something going on. He might have gotten away with hitting me this time, but I guarantee there will not be another one. Standing in the mirror I heard Derrick yell to whomever was at the door.

"Who is it?" He asked.

"Boy open this door! It Sheryl." His sister stated.

I heard the door come open and heard feet pouncing on the floor. I wasn't sure if they were headed this way or in the den, until I heard Sheryl yelling my name.

"Passion, where are you?" She called out.

At first, I was scared to say something. Then I responded, "I'm in the bedroom Sheryl!"

"Come up here! I have something I want to share with you all." She explained.

"Sheryl, I'm not feeling well. Go ahead and tell Derrick and he will tell me later." I shouted back at her.

I wasn't sure if Sheryl would go with what I said, or if she would come to see what was wrong with me. I waited to hear a response only to turn and see her standing right behind me.

"Passion, what the hell is wrong with your face? Did my brother do that? You bet not say yes!" She said in a demanding voice.

Crying and shivering, I couldn't help but nod my head yes. Sheryl grabbed my hand and escorted me into the den. Derrick was sitting on the sofa with his face inside of his hands. I guess he was now thinking about what he had just done to me. Standing me in front of Derrick. Sheryl said aggressively, "Did you put your hand on this girl? What the hell is wrong with you? You better tell me right now what's going on! And I mean right now."

"You're yelling at me! Ask her what's going on! Why were she at a hotel with Marlon last night." He proclaimed.

Sheryl turned her head to me in dismay with a surprised look on her face. She looked as though she couldn't believe what she had just heard. "Passion! I know he is lying, right?"

"No Sheryl! He is not lying, but whoever told him. They didn't tell him the real truth. See, last night I was in the exercising room asleep. The storm woke me up and I saw a shadow in the backyard. At first, I thought it was Derrick, but they were on the other side of the building. It frightened me. But as I tried to lock the door. Marlon opened it. He explained that he had been tracking Stephanie for a while, and she had left their home out of the blue. He became suspicious of her actions and wanted to find out what she was up too."

"Wait Passion! What does that have to do with you, and why was Marlon telling you all of this and not Derrick?" Sheryl asked still frowning up.

"Sheryl, I'm getting to that. He said he had already talked with him, and Derrick was going to go to a bar to get peace. Derrick had told him that I was in the exercising room asleep. After ringing the doorbell and getting no answer. He thought about I could still be asleep out back. Since Derrick went to get peace at the bar. He didn't want to disturb him. He figured I was the next person he could trust to accompany him to check up on Stephanie. He wanted someone to help keep things from getting out of hand if he found Stephanie cheating. See, he has a tracker on her car and knew exactly where she was. I couldn't say no to Marlon. You know during all the shit Derrick and I have been through Marlon has been a great friend. So, I went with him."

"Passion, are you fucking kidding us right now?" Derrick asked.

"No! I'm not. If you don't believe me. Call Marlon!" I said crying harder. "When we got there Stephanie was there. But the real kicker is who she was there with!"

At this point my tears started to dry up. I stared at Derrick directly in his eyes. I wanted to see his face when I say who she was accompanied by. This will tell me if he knows more than he lets on to know.

I went on to inform them both of whom was really at the hotel. "She was with Candice!" I said in a nasty tone.

"What did you just say, P?" Sheryl said.

"You heard me right Sheryl. They both were in a room together. Candice had on a negligee, while Stephanie was in her bra and panties."

"So, wait another minute. I'm trying to understand something. Derrick, how did you find out if Passion or Marlon never told you?" Sheryl asked.

"I got a call from Stephanie this morning, but her story was the exact opposite. She put it as though she caught Passion and Marlon at the hotel."

"So, you went off her word and just assaulted your wife? Derrick, boy I tell you!" Sheryl said while shaking her hand. "Derrick you out of all people, know how I fell about men abusing women. Especially, when you don't have the full story on what really happen. "

"Sheryl, you believe Passion?" He asked.

"Yes, I do! Because as much as I hate to say it. Passion loves you so much, that she would never defy you. There have been times I wish she would have, but she hasn't. You out of all people should know that. Oh, I forgot. You can't see that because your butt is always up to no good yourself. Therefore, you think she is too. Men kill me with y'all thinking patterns."

"Sheryl don't be fooled. Passion has some ways too. And you're correct I shouldn't have hit her, but just the thought of her being at a hotel with Marlon set me off. Wait, Sis! Come to think about it. I know you're not talking about my thought patterns. You need to stop comparing all men thought patterns. It's not all men faults your ex-husband thought patterns were deranged." He spoke sarcastically.

From the look on Sheryl's face. I could tell this angered her. She has always taken up for Derrick in all the mess he gets into, and the one time she took up for me. He reminded her of her ex-husband. Sheryl use to cherish the ground this man walked on. Until the day she came home and caught him having sex with their 15-year-old neighbor in her daughter's bedroom. I remember the first time I heard the story. I was flabbergasted by the details. Sheryl said as she entered their home. She heard moaning which grew louder as she walked up the steps. All she could think about was catching her daughter with a boy in her room. She could tell the sound was coming from her daughter's bedroom by the vibration on the steps. Her daughter's room was right at the top of the steps. As she had already prepared herself for such a day as this, because her daughter was now a teenager. But to her surprise as she swung the door open to confront her daughter, there laid her husband getting stroked by their neighbor. And when he noticed Sheryl standing there. He kept encouraging the girl to continue and the girl did as she was instructed. She showed no shame. Sheryl explained to me that she just stood there in shock. I recall her saying, she felt like Celie on the Color Purple when she first met Suge Avery. Sheryl said instead of assaulting them both. She left the house and went to get her daughter from gym practice and never went back. When Sheryl told me this story. I was kind of in shock myself because they both were employed as FBI Agents. She could have done real harm to him and got away with it. She didn't even tell the girl's parents or try to get him brought up on charges. Her defense was, she needed to get her daughter away from such a man as this, before he tried to seduce her. Sheryl left all her belongings and started over. She even transferred to another division. Sheryl has never been in a serious relationship since, and she never really talks about it either. Therefore, I can't understand why Derrick would bring it up at this time. I guess that's his way of trying to validate his actions towards me and make Sheryl feel bad about taking my side. But he needs to remember, the real validation is that he doesn't need to forget how Sheryl has always put his needs before hers. Sheryl still feels like she owes Derrick payback for him rescuing her from a rapist when they were younger. Derrick does not say anything about it since the rapist was their Dad. The scenario of catching her husband with her neighbor, must have also reminded her of the same scene when Derrick caught their Dad raping her. When Derrick first told me about it. He said he was glad when their father passed, and he did not shed one tear. Derrick also stated his feelings for his Mom was about the same. Especially, since she didn't believe them. The only person who believed them was Aunt Rose and that's why they are forever grateful to her. Aunt Rose took them away from their parents and raised them. Feeling like she owes them both, Sheryl still tries to show Derrick how much she appreciated his bravery against their Dad.

"Derrick, I dare you tell me how to think! Like I said before. Your thought patterns are just as jacked up as other men. The real jacked up pattern is, you felt the need to put your hands on Passion. I don't condone that on any day. Look at her face! If another officer were to drop by and see that. You would have added more fuel to the fire. Oh yeah! The real reason I stopped by, is to inform you all that Curtis Jones turned himself in this morning. He is being interviewed as we are speaking. Now, we can get some answers to why this all happened. But I'm not so sure now. Because how ironic is it that he turned himself in today after what took place last night. Passion, if you are telling the truth. He may be trying to cover up some more stuff. I just don't know about all this mess. The webs just keep winding farther and farther out adding more spiders to look at. I tried to keep from getting trapped into this mess. "Derrick, you better get with Marlon and Passion today to clear up the new web you added by putting your hands on her. Because if you're wrong and she is right. I don't see Passion letting this go so easily." Sheryl said as she made her way to the door and slammed it behind her.

Sitting across from Derrick staring him down made me ponder on what Sheryl had just said. Will I pay him back for all the pain he has caused me through the years? Should I call the police and report this physical abuse? Maybe if he goes to jail, he and Curtis Jones can finally meet up for real. Maybe they could share the same jail cell and hash out their differences. I totally agree with Sheryl on how this stuff just keeps going and going like the energizer bunny. Not only is she tired of it. I darn sure am. And if I can be honest with myself. It is only going to get worst.

I guess Derrick was thinking hard on everything now too. He got up and joined me on the loveseat.

"Passion, I'm sorry! But why didn't you tell me all that information at first?" Derrick advised.

"Because you never really gave me time to. You asked then reacted. Derrick it really doesn't matter now. You can't take those punches back and correct these bruises. Can You?" I said sarcastically.

"No, I can't. But I can try and get the real facts. I promise you that. I'm about to call Marlon and have him come over. Better yet, I'm calling him and Stephanie both. It's time we all sit down and discuss this shit. You said you are tired. I second that motion." He said as he walked out the den door into the backyard.

I rolled my eyes while watching him move swiftly out the door as he made his statement. My heart began to race, and my mind began to produce evil thoughts. Looks like clarity was about to enter our home. I can't wait to see who will validate who and who will continue to lie. We will all find out who really has been cheating with who? Or will we all remain trapped in our little secrets in order to cover up the relationships we all played a part in destructing. Funny thing is, I'm not saying I cheated with Marlon even if he stated it. I can only imagine if we confirmed what Stephanie already told Derrick. If he hit me off another's words. I can only imagine how he will act off my truth.

Getting up to go and finish doctoring on my face. I grabbed my phone and texted Marlon to make sure our stories matched. Because there is no way Stephanie would win this round. Especially, after getting my ass beat. I'm going to make sure pain knocks at her door today, just like it did me when I turned around and met Derrick's fist.

CHAPTER

9

Standing in the bathroom mirror, I rubbed medicine on my lips and my face to suppress any bruising from continuing. I also applied alcohol to whatever was aching, to try and help ease the pain. In doing this, I couldn't help but wonder how much pain Tay must have felt as she took her last breath. Janelle was right to a certain point. I was having thoughts about the person I called my best friend for years being gone. I wished I could turn back the hands of time. But I don't think I could turn them back far enough to remove everything her and Derrick have caused. Should I call Mrs. Anderson or just leave well enough alone. As my conscious continued to speak to me, I took a chance. I dialed Tayneshia's mother's number. My hands were shaking like I was in her presence.

"Hello, how can I help you?" The voice on the other side stated.

"Is this Mrs. Anderson?" I asked.

"Yes, Passion it is! Your name came up on the caller ID." She stated.

"Well, Ma'am. I'm pretty sure Janelle told you about our conversation the other day. But I had to call you to offer my condolences. I've had some time to think about the situation and I was wrong. I took my frustration out on Janelle. I just wanted to call to check on you and the rest of the family. I'm so sorry about the loss of your daughter despite the circumstances."

"Thank you so much! And I will speak for Janelle. Apology accepted. I explained to her that she has to see your point of view.

Janelle understands that better now. So, no harm should have been received on either side. And as far as how we are doing. We all are doing better than one can be expected to be. I appreciate your concerns. So, how have you been?" Mrs. Anderson asked.

"I'm ok. I could be better, but I'm trusting God. So, I will be fine. Well, Mrs. Anderson. I'm glad you all are fine, and I will keep you all in my prayers. I won't keep you any longer. Thanks for accepting my call." I said sorrowfully.

"You are more than welcome. Just in case you would like to attend her funeral services. It will be Friday at 1pm at the Visionary Funeral Home. I must inform you there will be no viewing of Tay's body. We don't want to let people view her like that." She said as I heard a sniffle or two.

"Thanks, but no thanks Mrs. Anderson. I still am not in any shape to face her. And you are right. I don't want to see her like that. I'm still trying to get pass the view of her I saw that day. So again, you all have my condolences and I'm praying for you all."

"Passion, I don't think you understand. Tay's body is not presentable. Whoever did this actually shot her in the face! It dismembered her facial features. I hardly even recognized my own child when they asked me to confirm that it was her. The reason I knew it was her was because of the two moles on the side of her neck." She said sobbing. "Mark checked out of reality and refused to do it. Therefore, I did. And Instantly, I decided not to show her body for viewing. We didn't even let her sons view it. Passion, I'm sorry. I need to get off now. Thanks for calling baby. Take care!" These were the words I heard as the call disconnected in my ear.

With my eyes closed tightly at this time. I immediately went into a silent prayer.

Dear God,

As I stand her with a hurting heart and a vengeful mind. I seek your guidance in this situation. Oh Lord in every situation! I call out to you to assist Tay's family in dealing with her death. Watch over her children and allow her husband to find peace in his heart. My God! We all have done some horrible things to each other and that is why I am praying. So please, do not allow any more harm to come out of all these unfaithful relationships. God, looking at where we are right now, only you can help us. We all are trapped in some dangerous emotions. Therefore, I pray that we do not act on our emotions any longer. We need you Lord! Please come see about us Father! In Jesus Name. Amen"

After administering this prayer silently. I changed my clothing that Derrick ripped while providing me with a punishment he thought I so deserved. Still anticipating Marlon's and Stephanie's arrival from our bedroom. I decided to rejoin Derrick in the den, only to discover they had already arrived. I guess I didn't hear them come in, due to being on the phone with Mrs. Anderson and praying. But they sure saw me come into the den, and what took place after that shocked us all. Marlon leaped from the chair in the corner toward Derrick's direction. He didn't say one word. He immediately started punching Derrick and using profanity. Derrick was clueless, just like I was when he punched me in the left eye earlier. The two men exchanged blows and wrestled repeatedly for about 15 minutes. Stephanie and I tried our best to break it up, but we both were tossed to the side. They had knocked over lamps, pictures, furniture, and much more. The only way this altercation finally broke up was that Marlon realized, he was going to hit Derrick's head on the bricks of the fireplace. I guess the realization in Marlon's mind, saved Derrick. We separated the two in different corners of the den, while they calmed down. If someone was peeping in the windows and knew who was married to whom. They might ask why I was in Marlon's corner trying to hold him back, and Derrick was in Stephanie's corner.

Finally, Marlon said a word while breathing hard, "Now Passion. Did Derrick do that to you?"

"Yes Marlon! But I'm ok!" I said pushing Marlon in his chest to keep him from moving forward.

"What the hell are you talking about? You're not ok! Your face is fucked up, and I know that shit hurts!" Marlon yelled.

Derrick responded, "Yes I did it! Because y'all think y'all are slick. Stephanie told me about last night!"

"Stephanie told you what about last night? She couldn't have told you the truth. Because if she would have. Passion's face wouldn't have been a target!" Marlon said angrily. "Fool, I caught her and Candice at the hotel last night together. Your wife went along as a support for me. Stephanie, tell him the truth!"

Derrick looked at Stephanie as though he wanted her to confirm his statement. But she didn't say a word. She just shook her head and cried. Derrick pushed her to the side and stared at her.

"Stephanie you bitch! You lied to me. Damn! Passion, I'm sorry!" Derrick said gazing in my direction.

At this point Stephanie fell to the floor and sat staring at the wall not saying a word. I didn't move away from Marlon. I felt so secure in his presence. It was like I was his zookeeper, and I needed to keep him tamed in the corner. I didn't want him to hurt Derrick any more than he might have already done. As for Stephanie and Derrick, I didn't care about either of them right now. I just wanted to make sure Marlon was ok. After he assured me, everything was ok, he and I walked over to be seated on the love seat, while Derrick sat on the edge of the coffee table.

"Okay! Now can we all talk civilized?" I asked. "I'm tired of all of this. We all need to come clean. But before we do. Are we all able to handle what the other may speak about the other one? No more playing games. I don't know if I can handle anything else. I'm so ready to release all of these trapped emotions. I know you all are too. Therefore, I'm going to go first!

"No Passion! I'm going first, because I don't know how long I can sit here and look at the both of them. And plus, every time I look at your face. I want to kill him!" Marlon said with tears whaling out of his eyes.

"Kill me, Marlon? I could say the same thing. I still really don't know why you and Passion were together last night. Y'all are saying one thing and Stephanie is saying another. And looking at you all, something is going on! How is it that my wife is sitting next to you right now?" Derrick stated strongly.

"Well, Derrick. She might be sitting next to me because I might be the only person in this room she can trust. So shut the fuck up and answer these questions! Since you seem to have so much to say now." Marlon advised Derrick. "Ok, are you and Stephanie messing around? Because, I have evidence to show it."

Derrick looked at Stephanie as she looked up at Marlon and said, "What are you talking about? I'm not messing with your wife!"

Marlon picked up the envelope that he had brought with him and started slanging pictures at Derrick and Stephanie. They both picked up various pictures and stared at them. The expressions on their faces let Marlon and I know they were surprised of what they were viewing.

"Nobody is going to say a word about the pictures?" Marlon asked.

Stephanie lifted her head and said, "Marlon, these pictures doesn't mean anything. They show me and Derrick talking, and some show us embracing each other. But to answer your question. We are not cheating with one another! You are wrong!"

But before she could continue, I intercepted her next sentence. "Then what are y'all doing? Oh yeah! Can it be that you all are engaging in a threesome affair? Let's not forget Candice from last night."

"No threesome Passion. If you and Marlon must know. I messed up and I couldn't go to Marlon about it. I felt ashamed and couldn't tell my husband. Especially, since we had a threesome with someone else and I enjoyed it. It was my mistake for going to Derrick and including him. Since he had dealt with Candice before, I felt better about talking with him about the mistake. Those pictures you all have, are in relevance to the times we met, to see how I could get out of the mess. I promise you both Derrick and I have never slept together. The only thing I am guilty of is, having strong feelings for him after confiding in him. I don't know if he has feelings for me or not. He has never made any advancements toward me. Marlon, I'm sorry but you're wrong about me and Derrick!" Stephanie pleaded.

"So, Stephanie! What was your mistake?" Marlon asked.

"My mistake is getting involved with Candice. It all started when I saw her at an event, I went to with my cousin Elise. She came up and we started talking about our old high school days. We started reminiscing about the times we use to hang out when she and Derrick dated. Our conversation led to us scheduling a time to chit chat about old times. We met a couple of days later and one thing led to another. After repeated meetings with Candice, she started to black mail me by saying she would tell you if I stopped messing with her. I wanted to stop fooling with her, because I finally figured out that she was using me to spy on Passion. When we would get together, she would always ask questions about her and Derrick. She even went so far to tell me she had a video of us, that she would put out if I stopped fooling with her. Please believe me! I've never slept with Derrick and I hate I ever slept with Candice!" She stated while crying.

We all just looked at her in amazement. Once again, Candice has trapped another victim. Now, I'm wondering what it is she has in store for me and why.

"Marlon! Stephanie is telling the truth. I wouldn't mess with your wife man. I've done some grimy things in my life. I've even messed with a lot of women, but I couldn't mess with Stephanie. Yes, I'm guilty of meeting with her without telling you, but I wanted to help her out of it. I know how Candice is. Hell, you know how Candice is yourself. She doesn't stop until she gets what she wants. Come on Marlon! You know that." Derrick said.

"And Derrick. Passion and Marlon are correct. I was at the hotel with Candice last night. I only told you that because I got caught. I was mad because Marlon told me to get out and he was taking my child. And when he and Passion walked off. I saw them holding hands. As I watched them leave. I just felt that the hand holding meant more than just a person being there for support. So, I made up the story of me catching them. If they are messing around. I don't have any proof. Passion, I'm so sorry I caused Derrick to hit you!" Stephanie stated as she got up from sitting on the floor and walked over to me.

Stephanie bent over to give me a hug, but I couldn't embrace her at this moment. I can't forgive her right now. She caused Derrick to hurt me. He did it on her account of lies about last night, and not from the truth that Marlon and I should be providing about our entanglement.

"Passion, saying sorry won't hurt the bruises and pain I've done to you again. But please forgive me!" Derrick stated as he walked over to me and grabbed my hand. I looked at Derrick with tears in my eyes. I stared at him because I was feeling ashamed. Only if he knew she was right. She was simply wrong about last night. Can I open my mouth and tell Derrick that Marlon and I had betrayed them both? I did state earlier about all of us being honest with one another, but I still feel justified for sleeping with Marlon because Derrick is a repeated cheater. I lowered my head to consult with my heart. Because I needed to speak what was present within it. I still loved my husband but had fallen for his best friend. Marlon and I shared yesterday some real feelings, but was I ready to share it with Stephanie and Derrick? I think not! I'm going to sit here and wait on Marlon's response.

Marlon started looking in my direction as though he was feeling my energy and said, "Derrick, I can apologize for my own actions today, and I will say sorry for putting your wife in my mess as well. But I'm not ashamed that we fought. There is no reason to beat your wife that way. Last night I wanted to do the same to Stephanie, but I just pushed her out of my way. I'm also guilty like Stephanie of having feelings. Yes Derrick! I have feelings for Passion because of all those times I've covered for you and played a role to cover up for you. I engulfed in strong thinking of what could be between her and I. And for you Stephanie. I'm supposed to be the first person you run to when something is wrong, no matter what it is. Damn! You did not even give me an option to engage in the activity with you and Candice." Marlon said sarcastically. "But for real. We are all here looking like fools. We all thought that the other ones were cheating with each other. But the real common denominator in this all, is Candice! I know she knew exactly what she was doing. She used us all in different ways to be in her little trap. It does not excuse how we all have acted, but it sure helps to know why. But when I get through with her ass. She will wish she never came for me and mine." He said staring at Derrick.

After listening to Marlon. I gave a big sigh. What I thought he was going to say, turned out to be the opposite of my expectation. He did a great job of smoothing over my feelings. Marlon was so convincing that Derrick got up and they embraced. But for Stephanie and I, there was no embracement. We both sat looking at them and then staring at each other. The look we gave each other was giving off signs that I knew she was lying, and she knew that Marlon was too. I guess our women intuitions had kicked in. Deep down in my spirit. I could feel the lying circulating in the room. Once again, we all held back our true feelings. Derrick and Marlon released from their bonding moment, and this time Derrick sat by me. He gave me a hug and kissed my forehead. It resembled when a mother kisses her child's wounds to make it feel better. At this point nothing Derrick does will make me feel better. It is still all his cheating that has us at a messy point. I can't help but wonder, when God will release me from being trapped in this marriage. Sitting in wonder mode, I started to sing aloud the gospel lyrics of, "Better Days are coming, I've seen good, and I've seen bad days. But I'm going to hang on in there, because better days are coming!" The more I felt the lyrics in my spirit. I had begun to sing louder. As I kept singing, Derrick joined in with me as he rubbed my back. We kept singing together until all of us were saying these words. I could feel the spirit of the Lord now swirling in the room. We were all crying and looking at each other. It reminded me of when Derrick and I use to sing in the church choir, when we first got married. No matter what sins we were doing at that time. We made our way to choir practice on Thursday and to church on Sunday mornings. But somewhere and somehow, we strayed away from the loyalty of the choir. Better yet, our loyalty to the church. Coming together today may not have brought about all the truths, but it sure got us to a place of coming together for a higher power and singing praises. But the real questions are. Do we believe in what we are singing? Will better days come from what we just shared and found out? Or will our days be filled with more destructions and traps that we have set for ourselves? All because we weren't totally honest with each other.

CHAPTER

10

Still humming the lyrics to the gospel song, Better Days. Derrick and I found ourselves engulfed in each other's arms. Our tears seemed to be holding battles of their own as they dripped own our faces. Once again, we had made our way back to each other. Unfortunately, we are still battling the reasons of why we are remaining trapped as Mr. and Mrs. Wilson. It was sad to look at Marlon and Stephanie as Derrick and I embraced. They were standing there looking at us in disbelief. I can only imagine the thoughts in their heads. Those thoughts probably reminded them of how they had just confessed their feelings for us and here we are wrapped in each other's arms. Derrick and I never confessed to loving neither of them. And now we are standing here as though our love just escalated more.

"Well, I see it is time I remove myself!" Marlon stated. "You all enjoy your make up time. I'm out of here."

Before Marlon could leave. Stephanie hollered out, "Marlon wait please! Can we talk about us and how to move forward?"

Marlon turned around with disgust wrote all over his face. He made a gesture with his hand as though he was saying forget you. Then he walked out of the den to the front door. We heard the door shut.

"Stephanie, I think you should follow your husband." I said with aggravation on my face. "And please, don't contact Derrick anymore. I think you all have been in contact too much. Who's to say you are not contacting him for your purposes as well as Candice. I'm still a little suspicious about all of this, but I love my husband and I'm going to fight for mine. I suggest you do the same."

Derrick remained silent as I spoke. But I could feel the trembling of his body as he continued to hold me. The trembling I felt was not that of nervousness, but I could tell it was that of should I move or remain in place. Looking out the corner of my eye. I noticed how the two of them were staring at one another. It was like they were giving off a signal of we will talk later. Stephanie grabbed her purse and left our house. After she had left, I started to pick up and place the furniture back in place. Derrick assisted me.

"Passion let's really talk. Was Marlon telling the truth?" Derrick asked.

"Was he telling the truth about what?" I asked.

"He said he had feelings for you, but I watched your body language. I believe it's the other way around."

I moved about an inch away from Derrick after we sat back on the sofa. I became fearful of how he may react if I agreed with him. My hands began to tremble, and I tried to speak, but nothing was coming out. Then finally I blurted out, "Yes Derrick. I have feelings for Marlon. You have got to think about all the times you left him to fill in your shoes. He became the one who shared my time and my world. Anyone could have caught feelings."

"Passion, I'm going to ask you this question and I pray the answer is no!" Derrick said with a sigh. "Have you ever slept with Marlon?"

"Derrick, I will only answer that question, if you admit you have slept with Stephanie?" I stated arrogantly.

"Yes Passion. I have. Now answer the damn question!" He said turning up his lips.

I hesitated at first, but then I confessed because he angered me with his answer. "Yes, Derrick I did!" I said as I flinched like a little kid would when their parent is getting ready to hit them.

Staring at me Derrick didn't move or say anything. This frightened me more. He didn't have a reaction to what I said. Something isn't right about this. He will hit me for Stephanie saying we were cheating together. But when I actually state the truth. He does nothing. I'm confused.

"Derrick, aren't you going to say anything?"

"No, P. I see your ass can't tell the truth for nothing. You only said yes because I said I slept with Stephanie. And plus, I can tell when you are lying. You answered too quickly. Dead giveaway." Derrick said as he kissed me on the cheek. "Come on let's get finished straightening up. Babe, I'm really sorry about earlier. Can I make it up to you? Let me take you to your favorite restaurant!" He asked.

"Really! I'm not sure about that. Did you forget about my face appearance?"

"Yeah, I forgot. It's not that bad though. Put some makeup over it. We really need to go someplace."

Agreeing with him, I gave a head nod. Derrick and I finished cleaning up. Then we started to change clothes to prepare for a night out together. While changing clothes Derrick received a call. After answering the phone, he exited the room. Whoever it was must have been important because he didn't want me to hear the conversation. Returning in the room he pulled out luggage from the closet and started to place items inside of it.

"Derrick, why are you packing a suitcase?" I said out of fear.

"Passion, we are going to leave town for a couple of days. This shit is really starting to make me want to act on my emotions." He said as he sat on the bed.

"What has happened now? Who was that on the phone?" I asked.

"That was Sheryl. She said Curtis told the investigators that he was paid to kill me. But he wouldn't tell them who. Just when I thought we could try to get our lives back to normal. Another bullet is being thrown. Funny thing is, I don't know who is doing the shooting."

"Oh my God! Where are we going to go? This is scaring me so much Derrick!" I said sitting beside him on the bed.

Derrick put his arms around me and said, "Babe, I got us! Just grab a couple of things and finish packing for me. I need to make some calls and then we are going to leave."

Quickly packing our bags, I couldn't help but wonder where we were going to go. Should I let Marlon know we were leaving? Or should I leave well enough alone? When Marlon left, he seemed to be upset with us all. But for some reason, I had a bad feeling about this trip. Especially, after what happen last night and today. Then there is the answer I gave Derrick about Marlon and me. He can say he doesn't believe it, but I know in the back of his head. He knows the truth. So, will he take me off and physical abuse me again. Or will this really be an escape from the person who wants him dead. I guess I really don't have a choice but to accompany him, since I am in the dark about many things right now. Giving Derrick's track record of cheating. I think he has finally acknowledged that he doesn't need to live up to it anymore. It has caused him a lot of things, but now it is causing him to fear for his life.

Grabbing what bags, I could. I walked to the garage where I found Derrick pacing and talking on the phone.

"Derrick, I'm done. Are you ready to go?"

"Yes Passion." He said as he spoke the last words to whoever, he was conversating with on the phone. "Is that all of the bags, or do I need to help you get the rest of them?"

"There are more inside. Which car are we taking?" I asked.

"Neither. Sheryl is almost here to take us to the airport." He explained.

"Wait a minute! So, we must fly some place? Ok, you have left out a lot. I thought we were just going on a road trip to get away. Now, you are talking about flying. I need to call my job and let my family know I'm going far away."

"No! There is no need to let anyone know we are going away. The ones who need to know will be notified. Sheryl will let them know and not to be worried. Trust me baby! I got you." He said looking at me as he walked back into the house."

I stood in the garage in a solemn mood wondering what the hell is going on. This is really getting fearful again. Derrick is leaving me out on something. First, he was upset about what Stephanie said about last night. He hits me. Then he has a physical altercation with Marlon and received a disturbing call from Sheryl. And just like that we are off on a plane. No, No! I'm not prepared for all of this. He needs to let me know exactly what's going on. Waiting on him to come out the house. I saw Sheryl pull in the driveway. She got out of her car and came to assist me with the luggage.

"Hey Passion. Are you ok?" She said while grabbing the bag out of my hand.

"Yes, Sheryl. I'm just scared, because your brother really is not telling me much. He told me what Curtis Jones said and we needed to get away. But now he saying we are flying some place. Do we really need to get that far away?" I responded.

"Well, yes! Because Curtis wouldn't give us who wanted him to kill Derrick. He is willing to go down for it by himself. He is putting it all on Derrick still messing with Candice, and he wanted payback anyhow. So, I suggested to Derrick that you all go on a little vacation. At least until we can investigate more. Passion, we can't forget whoever it is, went so far to kill your best friend and injured Derrick at the hotel already. What makes us think they won't try to kill the both of you to make sure he is dead? We don't' know! And being his sister. They may have tried once, but they won't get a second chance. I'm going to make sure of it. So, I've booked the flights, set up hotel accommodations, and a car rental. I even brought cash. We don't need you all to have to use any credit cards or banking information for purchases. I've come to the conclusion that, whoever we are dealing with are no dumb cookies. They are highly intelligent and maybe very financially stable. If they can pay for a hit. They mean business and we're going to show them we mean it too." Sheryl said looking deeply in my eyes.

Sheryl and I proceeded to put the luggage in the trunk. Derrick walked out with the rest of the bags and placed then in the trunk as well. He secured our dwelling before we all got in the car. Sheryl drove off rapidly, and we headed to the airport. While traveling, I kept thinking about where we were going. Will this really clear up anything? But knowing Sheryl's track record of making sure Derrick is ok. I'm sure it will. And to justify my thinking. My mind started replaying a conversation Sheryl and I had previously about Derrick's track records. She would often tell me that Derrick has always had some type of track record he wanted to keep up. Whether it was being known by his classmates as the most popular, the most athletics, and for sure the ladies' man. Then he went on to have a track record in the street life. The homies looked up too him for being the biggest street pharmacist to walk Tenison's Hoods. They also looked up to him for turning his profits into a legal profitable business. But, for me his biggest track record is for the one who is cheated the most on his wife. Sheryl would often remind me when I mention the cheating, that her brother was a good person. It's just he will try and get away with what he can. Especially, if giving the opportunity. She would constantly imply that, I let him get away with too much. And looking at the airport terminals right now, assured me that she was correct in a lot of ways. Why didn't I walk away after the doctor's office visit? No, I have always got to try and see the good in people and try to give them the benefit of the doubt.

Driving us around to our terminal. I notice Sheryl looking in her rearview mirror.

"Passion are you going to be, ok? I can see the worried look on your face. Sis don't worry everything is going to be fine. Trust me! I got y'all." Sheryl stated.

This caused Derrick to turn and look at me. "Passion, I told you we are going to be alright. I know I've messed up over a thousand times. Now, just trust me this once. I promise you when we get back everything will be ok." He said while turning back around and opening his door to get out of the car.

I didn't answer neither of them. I got out of the car and waited on him to finish talking with Sheryl. I looked around the airport terminals hoping this could be a dream, but unfortunately it was not. Derrick and I walked into the airport and went straight to the check-in desk. He gave our information and the attendant directed us to the correct terminal. Everything was flowing like clockwork and on schedule. Sheryl had dotted all her I's and crossed every T. We didn't have to wait to aboard the plane and the plane took off on schedule. Once we finally got comfortable in our seats. I asked Derrick where we were going. He looked at me with excitement and said, "To a place you've always wanted to go!"

I looked at him in his eyes. If it would have been under other circumstances. I might have had more enthusiasm about going someplace I had never been. But I wasn't too excited at this point. Therefore, I gave him a look of uncertainty.

"And where might that be?" I said sassily.

Derrick placed his hand over mind in my lap and said, "The Bahamas! Remember you wanted to go there after we got married. What a good place this will be to relax a little. Think about it. It's time we went someplace just the two of us for relaxation. Don't you think so?"

"Yes, it is! But Derick I must be honest. I don't feel good about this at all."

"Passion, babe please relax!" Derrick said jokingly. You've been wanting me all to yourself. Now you got it. I'm going to focus on you, and you can focus on me." He said as he leaned over and kissed my left cheek.

"Okay, I'm going to try. But it still doesn't feel right. And how long is this flight?" I asked.

"Well, P. Get ready for an eight-hour flight. Here, that's why I got you some ear buds from the house. We both will need to do a lot of things to occupy our time on this flight." Derrick stated as he handed me the ear buds.

"You sure are right about that!" I said laughing.

After accepting the ear buds from Derrick, I stared out the window looking in the clouds. What a beautiful view it was. I wished the view I was experiencing at this time, could be the view I saw daily. Therefore, I needed to embrace my view throughout the rest of this flight. While continuing to enjoy the clouds. I placed my ear buds in my ear and started to enjoy some soft music as well. I heard the voice of Sada singing:

> I won't pretend that I intend to stop living.
> I won't pretend I'm good at forgiving.
> But I can't hate you.
> Though I have tried.
> Ah.
>
> I still really love you.
> Love is stronger than pride.
> I still really love you.
> Mm.
>
> I won't pretend that I intend to stop living.
> I won't pretend I'm good at forgiving.
> But I can't hate you.
> Although I have tried.
> Mm-ah.

I still really love you.
Love is stronger than pride.
I still really love you.
Mm.

Sitting here wasting my time.
Would be like,
Waiting for the sun to rise.
It's all too clear things come and go.
Sitting here waiting for you.
Would be like waiting for winter,
It's gonna be cold.
There may even,
be snow.

I still really love you.
Love is stronger than pride.
I still really love you.
Love is stronger.
I still really love you.
Love is stronger than pride.

As the song came to an end. I found myself crying inside and out. I looked over at Derrick to find him fast asleep. Therefore, I hurried up and wiped my tears away. The words of the song reminded me that I still loved a man who has caused me so much pain, but on the other hand. I also must acknowledge that I may have also fallen in love with another man as well. So, am I crying for the man sitting next to me? Or am I crying for the man that's constantly fighting for my love. I wished I could call Marlon and let him know what was going on. I'm not even sure if he even wants to hear from me. But what I do know is when we land. I'm going to make sure he knows where I am and why.

It had been some time since we had boarded the plane, and I needed to use the restroom. I woke Derrick up so I could get out of our sitting area. He helped me out and quickly fell back to sleep. As I walked down the aisle to get to the bathroom of the plane. Two gentlemen on my right side caught my eye. One was a black male and the other one was a white male. The white man was sitting in the outer seat and the black man was seated on the inside. They both had on shades and baseball caps. But what was so ironic about the two men was, they resembled someone I knew, or had seen before. When I got closer to their aisle, they must have noticed me too. Because the black man leaned over as though he was looking for something on the floor, and the white man placed a magazine closer to his face. I kept walking and glancing in their direction to get a closer view of their faces, but I was unable to see them. I went on in the small restroom and quickly came out hoping on my way back to my seat. I could get a better view of them, but when I looked in the direction as before both seats were empty. This really made me uneasy. Where did they go? Because we are on a plane. I guess they went to the restroom or something. My conscious started speaking to me and reminding me that no one knew we were leaving accept Sheryl. So why would I know anyone on this plane. Therefore, I must do as Derrick had advised me and relax. I didn't want to awake him again, so I stepped over his legs and sat down. Wanting to reassure myself about the gentlemen. I turned around to see if they had sat back down. Only to discover they were seated, but in opposite seats that I originally saw them in. I still couldn't make out who they were, but I have a gut feeling they knew who we were, because they are trying to cover up their identity. They surely didn't want me to know who they were. I turned around wondering if I should awake Derrick and tell him about the men. Or should I just leave it alone. I don't want to bring up something that actually maybe nothing. Therefore, I'm going to mind my business, admire the clouds, and continue to listen to Sada.

CHAPTER

11

Watching the clouds disappear and seeing the blue ocean waters, let me know we were coming upon our destination. I finally saw the airport runway and started to get excited. I could see the beautiful trees and gardens. I was so excited that, I touched Derrick's arm to get him to look at what I was seeing. He leaned over and said, "We are here. Let the fun began!"

Preparing to exit the plane and to begin our vacation, we listened quietly to the flight attendant give instructions on exiting the plane. Derrick and I followed the instructions and proceeded to the exit entrance once the plane landed. Getting off the plane, I looked around to see if I could see the two gentlemen, but there was no trace of them. We walked inside the airport and retrieved our luggage. While gathering the luggage, I noticed the white male I saw on the plane. Our eyes met and I could now see his facial features. It shocked me. It was the man that came into the office at The Junction Restaurant. He looked me in my face and gave a nod. He retrieved his luggage and walked away. My heart began to beat faster, and I stood with my mouth open in disbelief. I started to think about the statement Marlon stated that day. He said to remember our conversations. Was he giving me certain clues to events to come? Or did he just want me to remember our time together. I could not say anything to Derrick right now, because he would find out I was there with Marlon. Therefore, I moved closer to him. Derrick was speaking with a man about getting us transportation to the hotel.

"Babe, come on the rental car is out front." Derrick said. "Passion are you ok? You look as though something is wrong."

"No! I'm ok Derrick. I'm just a little tired from the flight." I said quickly to detour his attention from my looks.

We walked out the airport and got into the rental car. The car was different. It was the opposite of our cars back home. The passenger seat was on the left side and the driver's seat was on the right. The funny thing was, Derrick was excited to drive. It was a new adventure for him. We drove off like we were driving off in the sunset of a new love.

We arrived at the hotel, and it looked like a mansion with different houses inside of it. There were butlers awaiting us at the driveway. They took our luggage and escorted us inside. We checked in and went straight to our room. The hotel room resembled a little apartment. There was a living area, dining room, bedroom, and a kitchen. The bedroom was cozy with drapes surrounding the bed and it had sliding wooden doors to lead to an open patio. The ocean came up to the end of the patio. But what fascinated me the most was the bathroom. The bathtub was made of crystal and was obstructed into an oval shape. The shower was surrounded by crystal leave artwork that matched the crystal floor patterns. The floor appeared fragile. It would make one think that if you walked too hard, everything would break. All the furniture was in white linen with silver accessories. It was just beautiful.

As I turned to walk back into the living room, after admiring the other part of our room. I didn't see Derrick. Walking back into the dining area, I spotted him on the patio. He was admiring the ocean. I joined him and placed my arms around his waist. I wanted to give Derrick a warm embrace. Because I almost felt secure in thinking, this trip may have been a great idea after all.

"Beautiful, isn't it?" I asked while rubbing his chest.

"Yes P! It is. Got me to thinking, only if we could stay here forever." He answered.

"Oh, I'm not sure I could live here forever, but I can enjoy myself while we are here. Anyways, how long will we be here?"

"Hopefully, only a week or two. Sheryl will call me and let me know how long in a couple of days." Derrick stated.

"Okay. Derrick did you let anyone else know we were leaving?" I said rolling my eyes behind his head. I wanted to know if he had contacted Marlon.

"If you're asking that question to see if I contacted Marlon or Stephanie. No, I didn't!" he said as he turned to face me.

"Well, I guess I can't put anything over on you." I said as I smiled while looking him in his face.

"Passion, I meant it when I said this is about us. I don't know who really wants me dead. Therefore, I can't take a chance of anyone knowing where we are. So please, don't contact anyone. I mean no one! Is that understood? I can't protect us if you're going to give out our whereabouts." Derrick instructed while pressing his body tighter into mine and staring me in my eyes. It was like he was giving me a warning.

"I hear you Derrick!" I said kissing him in his mouth while trying to distract him.

"Passion, I'm for real." He said as he kissed me back.

Engulfed in a passionate kiss. Derrick and I rubbed each other's bodies. He escorted me backwards into the bedroom, until we fell through the drapes onto the bed. Removing our clothing and massaging each other with our tongues, brought about the intimacy a place like this should bring on. Derrick and I was heading for the christening of the bed when he leaned over to get his wallet. He pulled out a condom and leaned back in the bed. As he put it on his manhood. I started to wonder; how long had he been carrying condoms in his wallet. Was he carrying them for our protection, or just in general? After he completed putting it on. He climbed on top of me and proceeded to insert his penis in my private area. Derrick stroked me repeatedly and he moaned with great passion that, he didn't even notice my interest had declined. My attention had turned to him having sex with other women. The ones I knew about and the others I didn't. I laid their disgusted and I wanted him to reach his climax. When I felt the strokes becoming harder and the moaning turning into a high pitch squalling. I became excited that it was finally fixing to be over. He reached his climax and rolled over onto his back. Laying there looking up in the ceiling, I saw a shadow flashed from outside on the patio. I looked over to see if Derrick saw it as well. But how could he. He was fast asleep. I shook my head and laughed. I thought about how my Mom use to say, "You will know if the sex was good, because the man will fall fast to sleep afterwards." Well, I guess it was good for him, but it sure was not for me.

I arose from the bed and closed the drapes to the bed on him. I picked up my clothing and was heading to take a shower when I saw the shadow go across the wall. It startled me and I put back on my clothing. I looked back at the bed to see if Derrick had woken up. But unfortunately, he was still asleep. Therefore, I walked to the patio to see if someone was out there. Looking straight in front of me and turning to the left of me. I did not find anyone or anything. But once I turned to my right side. My eyes open wider, and my lips parted. I got the biggest surprise a kid gets at his first birthday party. The only thing was, I could not scream and jump up and down. I quickly walked over to the right corner and whispered.

"What are you doing here?"

"I take it you are glad to see me?" Marlon asked.

"Yes boy! I've been wondering how I could contact you from here and see if you knew we was here." I said excitedly.

"Well, remember I told you to remember that day. Do you remember that?" He asked.

"Yes Marlon! I remember." I said trying to get him to hurry up with what he wanted to say.

"The guy that came in the office when we were at the Junction is an FBI Agent. He is one of the agents on the case. Sheryl asked him to come along to make sure you all were okay. She does not know that he and I know each other. He and I have been co-partnering on different business adventures for years. The Junction just happen to be one. He is also the investigator I had watching Stephanie. He called me and let me know the information Curtis provided and what was about to go down. So, I made the same plans. Passion, I meant it when I said I have strong feelings for you. After seeing your face earlier made me know that Derrick can't be trusted. I can't let him harm you anymore. Passion please don't let him know I'm here. He knows who Keith is." Marlon stated.

"So, Keith is the guy's name." I asked.

"Yes!" Marlon said.

Giving off a great sign of relief. I hugged Marlon and told him, "My lips are sealed. I feel so much better knowing you are here. But

I need to get back inside before he gets up. By the way, did you jump over the patios to get on ours?"

"Yes, I did! I saw Derrick out there and then I saw you when you walked out. And yes, I saw the little escapade you all just finished. Don't let it happen again either." Marlon said laughing.

"Really Marlon! You just stay close by and out of sight. Thanks so much for everything! I can go in and be at ease now knowing you're here too." I said kissing him on the cheek.

"You're welcome! We shall talk and meet up later." Marlon advised.

Turning and walking away I heard Marlon whisper, "Passion, I Love You!"

I turned to look back at him and he was gone. I walked into the doorway and turned around and closed the wood doors. I walked over and checked on Derrick to make sure he was still asleep and behold he was. I proceeded to the bathroom to shower but decided to experience a bubble bath in the oval tub. I turned the rushing water on and poured some bath beads in the water. As the water arose with steam. I couldn't wait to oblige myself in it. I lowered my body in the water and it instantly relaxed. Rubbing the bubbles back and forth along my arms. I thought about the two men on the airplane. Those two men were Marlon and Keith now that I think about it. They were trying to disguise themselves from us. And now, I'm wondering more about what Derrick is hiding, because Marlon said Keith was here on an assignment from Sheryl. Derrick must know he is here. But why is all this a secret from me. I don't know, but I'm going to play the little game he is playing. Especially now that I know some of the game. I continued to oblige myself in the bubble bath and thought about how interesting this vacation just got. The very person I wanted to know our whereabouts is here too.

As I finished up bathing, the words I love you rang in my head. Marlon sure seemed different than he was this morning. Looking at him on the patio reminded me of Dr. Jekyll and Mr. Hyde. One moment he wanted to kill the world or anyone in his way. And now he wants to be the loveable Marlon I met years ago. Thinking back now, why didn't he tell me the other day about the business venture with Keith? Exactly, what is he hiding as well? I believe he cares for me. I even think he loves me, but he has also been holding onto some secrets that he is slowly revealing. I got to keep my eyes on him as well. Reviewing his actions lately, Marlon is telling me he is done in his marriage and he is going to make sure I feel the same way. Unfortunately, I have strong feelings for him, but I still love Derrick. Marlon might be wondering why I can't kick those feelings. Well to be honest, I have also been wondering that!

Wiping off my body with a drying towel. I heard Derrick getting out of the bed. He walked in the bathroom and asked, "You took a bath without me babe?"

"You were asleep, and I didn't want to wake you. So, the answer is yes."

Reaching out and pulling me closer to him, Derrick responded, "I'm going to let you have this one, but the next bath or shower belongs to me. Do you want to order room service or go out for dinner?"

"It's a little late to be going out. Can we just order room service and watch a little TV? I would like to relax a little more." I said while still being embrace by the man who claims to be my husband.

"Okay, you got it. So, can you order us a meal while I take a shower?" Derrick asked.

"I got it. I hope you enjoy your shower as much as I enjoyed my bath!" I said as I walked out of the bathroom.

Entering the living area, I sat down on the couch. I located the hotel restaurant's menu and started to stroll through the menu items. I placed a call to room service while getting comfortable on the couch. Waiting for someone to answer the phone, I turned on the television. Once the clerk answered, I informed her that we wanted to place an order for dinner from their onsite restaurant. I explained to her that we needed two salmon entrees with grilled pineapples over rice, asparagus, and two classic Caesar salads. I also ordered a red wine to drink. The clerk asked if we would need anything additional, and I informed her that would be all. Hanging up the phone, I noticed a video of Jaheim and Terry Dexter playing on the TV. The video was Jaheim's song, "Remarkable." This song made me think about what Marlon said as I left the patio. Does he really think I am remarkable that he is in love with me? He must! He is here and not back in Tenison trying to work out his marriage. He flew all the way over here to make sure I am ok. Thinking about his feelings for me made me feel desirable and wanted. With me having feelings of being trapped in this marriage. I need real feelings of feeling wanted. I know my family and others think I am crazy for staying with Derrick, but I do love him. I can honestly say I'm having feelings for Marlon too.

"Passion, are you talking to yourself again? I didn't see you holding the phone." Derrick said as he giggled.

"I guess! Was I speaking out loud! I didn't notice me doing that." I stated turning up my lips as though I had said too much aloud.

Laughing Derrick said, "It was more like mumbling, but I could tell you are trying to convince yourself about something. Is there anything we need to talk about so you can clear your mind?" He asked.

"No Derrick! Just thinking about everything and how we can move forward after this is all over."

"Passion, stop worrying so much! Everything will be ok. Like I told you at home. I got us! Trust me, babe!" Derrick said as he sat on the couch with me.

Watching him sit down with just a towel wrapped around his waist. I nodded my head in his direction to give him assurance that I heard what he had just spoken. Did I really trust him? Hell no! My woman's intuition was telling me he was up to something. I just couldn't put my fingers on it yet. But best believe. I'm going to get to the bottom of why we are here, and why do we have to have someone watching over us. I want answers about what really happen that day at the hotel. Derrick has played me for a fool for too long. It's about time I trap him in his own mess and get my ultimate revenge. If I'm going to stay trapped in this marriage, I'm going to do it at my cost and no one else's.

Derrick started rubbing my feet when there was a knock at the door. He got up to answer the door.

"Who is it?" He asked while looking through the peep hole in the door.

"It's room service!" A male's voice shouted through the door.

Derrick opened the door and let the gentleman in. He pushed in the cart of food and lifted the dinner plate's tops to let us see what I had ordered. The aroma the food gave off, let us know it was prepared for our exquisite taste. Derrick thanked the gentleman and surprised me when he went to get him a tip. He gave him the tip and escorted him back to the door. After the gentleman left. Derrick and I made our way to the dining room table to have dinner. We chatted about this and that while eating. We even laughed and talked about our mishaps in our marriage. The meal was enjoyable, and I hate to say it, but so was the conversations. We cleaned up the dining room and placed the dishes back on the cart. Derrick pushed the cart outside the door and returned to the living room to join me on the couch. We continued to watch TV. It was amazing to see some of the same channels here in the Bahamas that we have back home. We ended up watching an old movie we had not saw in years. The movie called Steel Magnolia featuring Dolly Parton.

"Babe, I remember the first time you asked me to watch this with you. I told you, you were crazy. I'm not fixing to watch a bunch of old women getting their hair done." He laughed.

"Yes, I remember that too! But who ended up crying harder than me at the end of the movie?" I asked.

"Yeah! I must admit it. It made me cry thinking about how I use to have seizures when I was younger. I'm so glad I grew out of it. Seeing the daughter go through with what she did in the movie made me see how blessed I am. God spared me from epilepsy. Because some people don't make it just like Shelby didn't in the movie." Derrick stated staring at the TV and shaking his head.

Leaning forward to get closer to him as a means of support at this time, made me feel a sense of sadness for him. Derrick never talk about having epilepsy experiences. He would touch on the subject here and there, but never really gave many details about his experiences. That is why watching this movie with him always meant so much to me. It gave me a sense of understanding of some of the pains he went through as a child. I only wished I would have more of these times with him to better understand some of his cheating. But unfortunately, these times are rare.

Finishing the movie together had tired the both of us out. Having a great dinner and watching one of my favorite movies topped the evening off. We graduated from this day and went to bed. Instead of doing our normal of Derrick wrapping his body around mine. We did the opposite. I held him in my arms as we drifted off to sleep. I was the comforter of the night. I gave him a sense of security so that he could rest in assurance from the memories brought back from watching the movie. Because my assurance had met me on the patio an hour before. Wrapping my arms around Derrick made me wish I were wrapping them around Marlon for the night.

CHAPTER

12

A couple of days had passed since we arrived in the Bahamas, and I had not had any other encounters with Marlon. Most of the days consisted of spending time with Derrick and exploring the different places in the area we were vacationing at. I was beginning to wonder what Marlon was up to. I wasn't sure if his phone worked over here, and I didn't know his exact room number to even get any information. Therefore, contacting him seemed impossible. But to be honest, spending all this quality time with Derrick was bringing on a little peace in our lives. It was like when we first started dating. It was just he and I. We had long talks, took walks, and shared old stories. The only thing we were not engaging in was sexual activities. For some reason, I believed Derrick did not want this trip to be all about sex, but about us getting to a place of loving each other wholeheartedly again. Therefore, I must get my mind from what Marlon has going on and focus on my husband. Especially, if I wanted the marriage to work.

"Passion, I'm going to step out for a minute. I need to go meet someone. I will be back in about an hour or two." Derrick stated.

"Huh! You are going to meet who? Who do you know over here?" I asked. Knowing the whole time, he was talking about Keith the agent Marlon told me about.

"Oh, here you go P! Sheryl sent one of her agents over here to make sure we are safe while here. I'm going to meet up with him to see what's going on back home. That's it! Stop thinking negative."

"Okay, why didn't you say something about him days ago? All these secrets you're keeping. I don't like being in the dark about stuff. And plus, if you are just going to meet the agent, why can't I go?"

"Passion! You got to trust me! How many times do I have to say that? Everything has been going smooth with us for the last couple of days. I don't want to ruin that by whatever is going on back home. Let a man be a man! I got us into this, and I need to get us out of it. Here, take this money and go shopping or something. By the time I'm done. You should be as well. We will meet back here and do something together later. Okay!" He said handing me a roll of money.

Derrick did not give me a chance to answer. He walked out the door and slammed it. Little did he know? I really wasn't upset. I just wanted to know his whereabouts and a time frame so I could locate Marlon. Knowing he was going to meet Keith gave me a sense of security. I hurriedly got dressed and started the scavenger hunt to locate Marlon. First, I emailed him from my laptop. Secondly, I even tried disguising my voice and calling the front desk to inquire about a room number for him. And then, the bell went off in my head. It reminded me that his phone could work over here as well. I immediately grabbed my phone and dialed his number. Without any hesitation. Marlon answered on the first ring.

"Hello Passion! I knew you would be calling." He chuckled.

"And just how did you know that?" I said jokingly.

"Once Keith told me he and Derrick were meeting up today. I knew you would. Especially since it's been days of us speaking to one another." Marlon said.

"Well, I guess you do know a little about me!" I laughed. "So, where are you now? Can I come to your room?"

"I'm in room 132 on the other side of the hallway, and you know damn well you can come to my room. I've been waiting on this day to have you in here! "Marlon stated aggressively.

"Okay, I'm on my way! We only have about an hour or two. He left money for me to go shopping." I said grabbing my purse and room key while exiting the door.

I remained on the phone with Marlon as I walked around to his room. Finally reaching room 132, the anticipation that fluttered my heart was relieved. He had left the door cracked for me to go ahead and enter without knocking. I pushed the door open and saw the same similarities of our hotel room. I walked farther into the living area of the room expecting Marlon to be present. I still didn't see him. Therefore, I called out to him.

"Marlon, where are you?"

"Passion, I'm on the patio. Come out here!" Marlon yelled back inside to me.

I ascended to the patio. After arriving there, my eyes were impressed by the view of breakfast set up on a table for two. Marlon stood behind a chair he had pulled out for me to be seated. After I sat down in the chair, Marlon pushed me closer to the table and walked around to be seated himself. With google eyes, I batted them to let him know I was overly impressed. I was not even worried about being seen in the open with Marlon. All I wanted to do was to enjoy the moment.

"Marlon, what did I do to deserve all of this?" I asked.

"Nothing! I just wanted to apologize for my actions back home. I must admit it. I was upset when you didn't share your feelings for me, but I understood that you may have been afraid to. I kind of put myself in your shoes. If I would have got hit earlier. I would not have wanted to receive more abuse. So, take this as my offering for forgiveness." Marlon said as he reached over and grabbed one of my hands.

"You don't owe me any apologies! I was flattered that you took up for me. And I was even more flattered when you told the truth about your feelings. But I do have to ask you. What about you and Stephanie?"

"Passion, have you ever wanted something to be permanent, but you finally realized it was designed too only be temporary? See Passion, it took me years to see Stephanie only married me because we had a child together. She used to say when we were dating, that she didn't want to have a child and raise it by herself. Over the years, her actions started to match her theory for having children. She was not going to raise our daughter by herself. And to be honest, my feelings started reacting to her actions. So, to answer your question. There is no more Stephanie and me. I'm going to raise my daughter, so she won't have to raise her by herself. I had already started the steps of the divorce before we went to the hotel. That just made me put a rush on things. I have been in contact with my lawyer since I've been over here. I've had him to go ahead and serve her with the papers. Hopefully when I get back, she will have received them and signed them. I've already talked with my daughter and she is clear on what's about to happen. She even confirmed that she would rather be with me than her mother. P, I'm ready to move on and be happy. What about you?" He asked.

Marlon left me in shock by what he had just said. He wasn't playing games about his marriage. Better yet, he was playing around about his feelings. He had taken all the right steps to get his freedom and get back his happiness. Shit, he is even willing to be a single father raising a teenage girl. And that is rare for men of today. But the question he is asking me right now about what I am going to do. I really don't know how to answer it at the moment. I haven't reached a point of totally walking away from Derrick. Hell, I still love him even though he has caused me so much pain. But I love Marlon too. Looking at Marlon right now trying to speak a true answer. I couldn't. The words wouldn't even extrude from my lips. The only thing that came from me at this time, was the tears that started to drip down my face.

"Passion, you don't have to answer right now. I can see from the tears that your temporary status is still a permanent one inside of your heart. That's why I've always wished I would have met you before Derrick did. You love him so much even after all he has done. I hope he finally realizes that and changes his ways. Oh yeah! Just because I know you still love him will not change how I feel. I'm not going to give up either. Because I know somewhere in that big heart of yours. I have a piece of it too." Marlon spoke as his tears started to run.

I reached over and grabbed his other hand as well. We sat for a moment in silence just admiring each other as we both cried.

"Marlon, I will confirm something you said. You do hold a big piece of my heart! I'm just so confused and I wouldn't dare lead you on knowing, I still love him very much. I've been praying that God hurry up and show me if I'm supposed to leave or stay. Hopefully, that time will come soon."

"Are you serious right now Passion? In my opinion, God has already showed you plenty of times. You are simply scared to move on. I wish I knew why though!" Marlon said with a frown.

"I don't know why Marlon. I keep wanting it to be God too, but sometimes I believe it is the devil too. You know he does things to us as well?" I said trying to justify my belief on why I'm staying.

"If you say so! Let's enjoy our breakfast before you have to leave me." He said laughing.

Marlon and I completed our breakfast along with feeding each other the fruit off our plates. We remained on the patio after breakfast for a minute admiring the view of the water. Watching the waves move up against the patio, I lost myself in the comfort of Marlon's presence. He stood behind me holding both of my hands and occasionally kissing my neck. This made me close my eyes and have wishful thoughts of us making love again. Why did I still love Derrick? Here stands a man wanting to give me the peace and happiness I deserved. He has repeatedly showed me he would do anything and everything for me. Reciting the serenity prayer in my head. I turned to face Marlon to speak it aloud.

"God, I come to you in the presence of Marlon. Lord, Grant me the serenity to accept the things I cannot change, the courage to change the things I can, and the wisdom to know the difference." I uttered as I finished with a kiss on Marlon's lips.

Marlon glared down at me and said, "Come inside with me. I want to show you something I received the day I left for the trip."

Following him inside still holding his hand. I began to wonder what he needed to show me. I hope it is good news. Escorting me to the couch, he made sure I was comfortable first before he walked away. Marlon went into the bedroom and returned with a paper in his hand. He sat on side of me and presented the paper to me.

"Here, I think you need to see this!" He said as he put the paper in front of me.

I took the paper and started to read it. After carefully reading the document, it appeared to be results from testing performed on a person in question of having HIV. Getting to the bottom of the paper the word negative glared out to me in red. Yes, it was great news! I looked up from the paper and turned to give Marlon a big hug. Marlon had received the results from his HIV testing, and he was negative.

With great excitement I yelled, "Yes!"

"I thought you would be happy about that. I know I was." He spoke.

"So did Stephanie get tested?" I asked.

"I'm not sure Passion. I went by myself when you and Derrick told me. I had to know since we had slept around. That's why I told you to stop with the escapades you and Derrick where doing. You're negative and so am I. We don't need to put ourselves in anymore risks." Marlon stated.

"Boy, we use protection! I actually can't believe he initiates it when we have sex." I answered. "Marlon, do you still feel Derrick and Stephanie have something going on?"

"Passion, I don't know. Those pictures just don't say to me that he was only supporting her because of her involvement with Candice. Oh yeah, I didn't share the information what Keith told me about Curtis and Candice! Looks like they have been divorced for years. They have been trying to make it work off and on through the years, but never really got back together again as husband and wife. When Curtis turned himself in. He told the investigators he hated Candice as much as we do. So, his motive for trying to kill Derrick had nothing to do with her. He also told them when he got to the room everything had already transpired. He stated the girl was on the bed in a pool of blood and Derrick was lying on the floor unconscious. Seemed as though someone had beat him to the punch. Keith told me they asked Curtis who hired him then. He said he never met with the person. He became interested by an email he received talking about Candice and Derrick cheating behind his back when they were married. He said he received repeated emails throughout the years from an unknown source. They would always email him. Every conversation and money transaction would happen via the emails as well. Curtis even held on to the checks that was mailed to his PO Box for payment. Funny thing is the checks were from a bank account that turned out to be fraudulent. Curtis was glad he didn't perform the act, because he would have done a job with no payment. See, that's why Derrick thought Curtis did it. Evidently, Derrick played unconscious and saw Curtis when he came in. So, after Sheryl got wind of the information. She thought it was a good idea to get Derrick to a safe place until they could gather more information on this mysterious person."

"Humm! I guess that is what Keith wants to talk to Derrick about today?" I asked.

"No, Sheryl already told Derrick that. That's why he agreed to come to the Bahamas. Keith wanted to update him on what he found out yesterday." Marlon replied.

"I hate being in the dark! Especially, when my life is estate as well." Derrick just keeps saying, "Let me handle it!" "How the hell can he handle it, when he doesn't even know who it is his damn self? Uhhhh, this shit makes me mad!"

"Calm down babe! That's why I'm telling you all of this so you will know. Keith was informed yesterday that they were able to track some of the emails Curtis received. Looks like the emails came from an IP address from your hometown of Garden City. After further investigation. The emails were being sent by Tayneshia email address." He said looking side eye at me.

"Tayneshia!" I screamed. "Wait! Wait a minute! Remember I received a similar email at work after all this happened. But it was saying Derrick and Stephanie were cheating together. It was from an unknown source too. But Tay couldn't have sent that one. She is dead now!" I spoke.

"I don't know P! Something strange is going on. We just got to wait it out and see what. Hell, that's also another reason I left too. Who knows? I could be a target too." Marlon stated as he rubbed my leg. "By the way have you talked to any of Tay's family?"

"Yes, I received a call from her sister Janelle. That call didn't go well at all. Therefore, I reached out to her mother to apologize for my actions. We talked and she assured me everything was ok. She did say Mark, Tay's husband, was having a hard time dealing with it, but everyone else was doing good as expected."

"So will you be attending the funeral services?" He asked.

"Hell no! I might just attend only to fight the dead. No, I'm good. I really don't think I can face Tayneshia even knowing she is dead." I said in a disrespectful way.

"Passion, I believe it is a good idea if you don't go. You just never know. Mark could be the one who made this all happen. Looking at the evidence coming out now. We just don't know."

"Marlon, why was I just sitting here thinking the same thing? Emails coming from Tay's email address. He is having a hard time coping. And he has always been strange to me anyway."

"How so, P?"

"Well, he would always sit around and stare. He would do the kind of staring that would freak you out. Every time I would catch him staring at me. He would try and turn away to make me think he wasn't looking at me. Mark is standoffish and watched Tayneshia like a hawk staring at its prey. I remember one time we went out to a gentlemen's club with some of our friends. He quizzed her before we left, and even harder when she returned. Tay told me that night when she got home. He made her lay on the bed and undress. He checked her private parts to see if she had intercourse while gone. He went so far as to stick his fingers inside of her and smelled them. Yuck! Where do they do that at? I really don't think Mark cared for me much either. Whenever I was around, and he would become aggressive with her. I would always try to diffuse the situation. Mark constantly put Tay down. She often let his views of her, be the reason she felt she was not beautiful. Tayneshia would tell me that repeatedly. Sometimes I think that's probably why she went after Derrick. You know how Derrick will try and make you feel good about your flaws to get what he wants."

"Humm, Passion! I hate to say this babe. But don't Mark and Tay sound a lot like you and Derrick?" Marlon stated.

"No! Why would you say that?" I asked Marlon with enthusiasm.

"Passion, Derrick has been being aggressive with you. He tries to turn his mistakes on you, and he also tries to make them your fault. He refuses to acknowledge that he committed them in the first place. Derrick watches your every move like a hawk lately. The only thing he hasn't done, is check your private areas. Or has he?" Marlon quizzed.

"No Marlon! He hasn't. And I guess you are a little correct. I have never looked at it from that point of view. Wow! Great observation Marlon!" I said as I got up off the couch and walked to the patio door.

Marlon walked over to me and put his hands on my shoulders. "Passion, I'm sorry! I wasn't trying to make you feel bad. I just wanted you to see how Derrick is doing you. I just want you to see him for what he is! I'm not just saying this because I'm in love with you either. I just want you to wake up before you end up like Tay! I don't know what I would do if something happened to you." Marlon explained as he twisted my body to make me face him.

Marlon and I kissed vigorously until I heard my phone ringing. I pulled away from him in order to retrieve my phone. I knew it was Derrick calling. Therefore, I had to answer the call so he wouldn't get suspicious.

"Hello!" I answered.

"Babe are you enjoying yourself shopping?" Derrick asked.

"I didn't go shopping. I decided to just roam the streets and to enjoy the scenery. I wanted to clear my mind of somethings. I really didn't feel like shopping today Derrick."

"Well, we are about through talking here. So, I'm fixing to finish up this drink and head back to the room. Would you like me to pick you up anything?"

"No Derrick! I don't need anything. I'm going to head back to the room too. I will meet you there."

"Okay, P! But what's wrong? You never really call me by my name unless you're angry or sad about something."

"There is nothing wrong really. Like I said, I've been trying to clear my mind about some stuff! I'm a little sad, but I will be ok. You just hurry back and see if that will make me feel better." I said trying to make Derrick think I missed him.

"Ok, Babe! I'm on my way now. When I get there be ready to go back out. I want to take you some place so we can have a little fun." He advised.

"Alright, I will be ready." I stated hanging up the call.

"Well, Marlon. I must go. He is on his way back to the room. I need to get a head start to be him back. Thanks for breakfast and the conversation. It was wonderful as usual." I said while kissing his lips again.

"I hate to see you leave, but in due time I won't have to watch you leave. I promise you. You will be mine! I put that on my life." Marlon said as he walked me to the door.

Giving Marlon a goodbye kiss. I walked out of the door and moved quickly to the other side of the hotel. Just as I was unlocking the room door. I saw Derrick coming down the hallway in the corner of my right eye. I continued to open the door and entered the room. I left the door halfway open so he could enter as well. Derrick came in and locked the door. He walked pass me and headed straight to the bathroom.

We both started grinning at one another. We both knew what his rush was all about. He had been drinking and needed to release his bladder. While Derrick released his bladder, I sat at the dining room table staring out the patio door. I couldn't help but think about what Marlon said. Are we just like Tay and Mark? Will I end up like Tay? I guess only time will tell. Who's to say? It could turn out that I end up like Mark, and Derrick ends up being like Tay!

CHAPTER

13

"Babe, was your walk enjoyable? I hope you got to see a lot more of the island." Derrick stated as he sat down at the dinner table with me.

"It was pleasant. I got to clear my mind a little more. So, how was your visit?" I asked.

"Passion, it went really well. I received more valuable information on why some of this happened. I met with Sheryl's friend on her team. His name is Keith. He let me know that Curtis was paid to kill me, but once he arrived. He saw that it had already been done. Curtis admitted to being at the hotel, but he advised that he was not the shooter. He also informed me about some emails going around to different people, and the emails are being submitted from Tayneshia's email address. It threw me for some loops at first, but I understood it as he kept talking. What's crazy is, I didn't know Candice and Curtis are divorced. After hearing all of this, I started thinking about Tay's husband. But I didn't see no one else at the hotel. Passion, I'm still confused, but now I do have a little more information to go on. I wish I could speak with Marlon. I need him to check on some things for me. But I know he is still angry with me, and I doubt if he will do anything to assist me! Therefore, babe don't be mad at me, but I might have to call Stephanie to help me out." Derrick stated while looking at me.

"Really Derrick! That's what you've come up with now? You been wanting to contact her anyhow. I thought we were not telling anyone where we are? But you are going to call Stephanie, who maybe still in contact with Candice. We don't really know if Mark is involved in this or not. I don't put anything past Candice though. Better yet, Stephanie! But you do what you want. You've always done it anyway. What I think doesn't matter! Because if it did, we wouldn't be sitting here now!" I said getting up from the table to walk off.

Derrick jumped up and grabbed my arm just as I was about to pass him. With a strong jerk, I fell into him. "So, what now? I'm about to get hit in my right eye for speaking my truth!"

"No Passion, I'm not going to hit you! Please sit back down. I need to talk to you about something else." He stated.

I yanked my arm from the grip Derrick had on it and walked into the living room. Derrick followed me.

"Okay, I have another confession. We said we were going to be honest about everything moving forward in our marriage. Right?" Derrick said awaiting a confirmation from me, but I didn't answer. I just stared at him.

"Well Passion. Oh my God! How can I say this without you flying off the handle? Keith told me I must go ahead and tell you now, because it's going to come out sooner or later. Babe! I have another child besides DJ." He said holding his head down.

"What did you just say? I know I didn't hear you say you have a child outside of DJ! And I know it bet not be with Candice!" I said as I stood up over him.

"P, please sit back down! I'm fixing to tell you." He said as tears started to fill up in his eyes. "Boy, this is hard to say. The night before we got married. I slept with Tay and supposedly she got pregnant at that time. She didn't tell me until about two months ago. Only, because the child got sick and needed some blood. Mark was going to donate blood because the child has a rare blood type. He thought he might be a match since he was the father, but it was determined he wasn't. So, Tayneshia called me and then spilled the beans about me being the father. I argued with her at first, because I had told her about two weeks before that, that I didn't want to see her anymore. But when she told me the child's blood type was the same as mine. I agreed to take a blood test. The test came back positive for me being the father. Do you remember I told you I needed to take a trip for business for two days?

Well, I went to Garden City and donated blood for the child. Mark and I had some words while I were there, and he promised he would get me back. I never expected him to try and kill me or Tay. I was thinking more on the lines of him telling you about the child or trying to sleep with you. So, you see, that's why now I can see why he could have been involved in all of this." Derrick stated while holding both of my hands down and looking into my eyes.

With tears streaming down my face. I barely heard the rest of Derrick's opinions about Mark's involvement. I was still stuck on the fact that Tay's son is Derrick's. Marlon was absolutely correct. Derrick and I are actually just like Tay and Mark. It's just I have been the only one in the dark about some stuff. I can't help but wonder now, if Marlon knows about the child. The trip to the Bahamas just turned for the worst for me. This asshole just dropped a bomb on me, and there is nowhere for me to run. I must stay here with him trapped until, I can get back home and do otherwise. Not speaking one word, I stared at him. I wanted him to finish his conversation quickly. I just kept giving him the evil eyes.

"Babe, please say something! I know this shit is unbelievable. Yes, I fucked up bad with this one. I can't blame you if you leave me after hearing all of this!" Derrick said gripping my hands a little harder to keep me from striking him.

"Derrick Wilson! You are correct. I want out. I can't do this with you no more. The sad thing is, I got hit for a statement Stephanie made about me sleeping with Marlon. But you have a whole baby with my best friend! Humm, so since we are being honest. Yes, I slept with Marlon. The night you were in the hospital. Yes! I have strong feelings for him and after hearing this. I probably will fuck him again on GP!" I said angrily hoping it would make him upset.

"I deserve that Passion. I already knew you slept with Marlon. I just played it off to ease your mind. We've both fucked up in this marriage, but I still want our marriage to work babe. I know I started all of this. Like I told you. I'm going to make all of this right."

"How Derrick? You now have a son! A son that calls me Godmother. Oh my! Why me Lord! What did I do to deserve this? And wait! If you had a blood test done two months ago. Then when we received the results at the doctor that day. You should have already known about being HIV positive before you got shot. You knew, didn't you?" I asked.

Sighing heavily Derrick let go of my hands. He moved backwards on the couch and put his hands over his face. Then he sat back up and said, "Yes, P! You're correct. When the test came back, they told me, I was positive."

"So, was she positive too? And what about the child? Because you donated blood to him. You bastard!"

"Tayneshia was positive too. The child didn't get my blood, because of the test results coming back positive for HIV. Damn! I'm sorry Babe."

"Now the real question is, Does Mark have it too? Or do you know that?" I asked.

"Yes, Mark is positive too! I learned that when I was there those two days. Tayneshia found out two years ago and never told Mark or I for that matter. It wasn't until we both were tested to donate blood that we found out. Mark is blaming me for it and not Tay. But I'm not to blame, because you or the other women I've been messing with came up positive."

"So, you are telling me now, that Stephanie and Candice know and have been tested?"

"Yes, Passion! I told them and they got tested. They showed me their results. Stephanie told me she thinks Marlon got tested too, because a doctor called the house for him. She is unsure of his results though. Do you know if he is or not?"

"Marlon is good! He told me his test was negative. It's funny for sure now! You both got what y'all deserved. I pray God forgives me for the feelings and thoughts I'm having right now. But I wish I could congratulate whoever did the act at the hotel. One down and just maybe one more to go!" I said with a smirk on my face.

"P, cut that shit out! No one deserves to die because of cheating. Hell, if that's the case. Marlon and you deserve the same thing. We all have done some grimy things in our marriages. Repentance needs to be upon us. So, I am going to let you think and say as you please right now. Hell, vent, and get it out. You want to hit me, then go ahead. But at the end of the day. Somebody wants me dead, and we don't know if they are gunning for you as well. But before, I let them hurt you or me. I'm going to find out who they are and do my best to stop them. Babe, I love you whether you believe me or not." Derrick yelled out while crying.

I didn't care about him yelling I love you, and I even wasn't focusing in on all of the HIV results. And who cares about who shot them, or who maybe after us. That just didn't seem to matter much right now. Especially, since Derrick just dropped the bomb that Tay's son Lenton is his. All I could think about was Linton. Does he know that Derrick is his father? Lenton has always been special to me since birth. He was born with autism. I remember when she called me to say something was wrong with him. Tay was afraid because Lenton was learning slower than the other kids. He would become angry for no apparent reason as well. He didn't care to interact with other kids much. Lenton couldn't speak words clearly, but he sure loved numbers. I would often check on him, and I would go to take him different places. Because of Lenton's autism. He was remarkably interesting to me. He is a big hugger just like me, and he always knows when I am feeling down. He would squeeze me and say his favorite number which is nine. I never understood why nine was his favorite number. It was not until, I read in an article about the number nine. The article said that the number nine symbolizes love and faith but could also symbolize karma and spiritual laws. So, I took it's meaning from Lenton to be his love and faith for me. All because, Tayneshia was ashamed of her own child. She confided in me by saying, "It was embarrassing when they would be in public, and other people would stare at him for his behaviors." Therefore, I tried to do things with him because I wasn't embarrassed by Lenton. It's crazy how I will have to pray now that the love Lenton and I share remains genuine. Not on his part, but on mine, because he is really my stepson. I don't want to hold any grudges against Lenton for the actions of Tay and Derrick. He is innocent. This is bringing me more pain within my heart just to think about it. I had to come all this way to finally get some of the answers for everything that has been happening. It's getting harder by the minute to sit back and to just let things unfold. I can only imagine what I may hear next.

Remaining sitting on the couch. Derrick and I just sat looking at each other. He kept looking off in order not to keep having to look me in the face. For a minute, we were engaging in a stare contest. I can only imagine the thoughts that were racing through his head right now. Derrick hesitated, but eventually started to talk again.

"Do you have anything you want to say?" he asked.

"Nope! I'm going to sit right here, and let you tell me the rest of what I think you need to be honest about."

"And what is that Passion?" Derrick asked in a solemn tone.

"Stephanie and Candice! Do you have children with them too? Have you all had a threesome? Were you at the hotel that night when Marlon and I came there? Oh yeah! Did Stephanie come to the hotel the day you and Tay was there? I want to know all about that!" I said shaking my finger in his face like a high school girl.

"Passion, can you really handle the truth about all of that? Because if you can, then let's talk about it." He said shrugging his shoulders.

"I asked! Didn't I."

Derrick chuckled as though my responses were pissing him off. Then he started off by saying, "Ok, here it goes! There are no other children to my knowledge. Threesome with Stephanie and Candice, Hell no! And no, I wasn't at the hotel with them that night. I was really at the bar having a drink by myself. Yes, Stephanie came to the Shamrock Hotel that day. But not to confront me. She came because she and Candice were supposed to meet there that day too. When she saw Tay and I, she told me I was wrong for messing with Tay. Tay snapped back at Stephanie and that's why they were arguing. I made Tay go in the room while I talked with Stephanie. She started talking about Candice saying she was going to tell Marlon about them. Stephanie wanted my advice on what she should do. I told her to call me later and I would see how I could help her. Stephanie left and I went in the room. When I got in there. Tay was across the bed with blood gushing out of her chest. I didn't hear any shots fired or nothing Passion! Then suddenly, someone came from the bathroom and started shooting at me. All I remember was hitting the floor. I passed out for a minute and when I started to come around. I saw Curtis Jones standing over me. Therefore, I closed my eyes back and held my break to make him think I was dead. Not long after that you came in, and that's why I told you to leave, because I wasn't sure he or whomever was gone." Derrick said getting louder in his voice.

After hearing what Derrick had just said, my paralegal skills started to kick in. I couldn't help but follow up with some questions. "Derrick, if what you're saying is true. Do you think maybe Candace was already in your hotel room and Stephanie was a diversion to get you and Tay off guard? And just maybe Curtis was watching Candice and that's how he ended up there too."

"No Babe! Keith said Curtis was paid to kill me and was sent to the hotel. So that can't be it." He explained.

"Not necessarily Derrick! Think about it? What if Candice somehow got Tayneshia's email information and started sending the emails to make it look like Tay was doing it. You said her and Curtis are divorced. So, she could have tried to put him in the mix to get back at him. She also has Stephanie under her control now by black mailing her. Therefore, she could have made Stephanie get information through our law firm on everybody."

"Passion, I never even thought about it that way!"

"Derrick, think back and tell me if the room had an adjoining door?" I asked.

Looking confused Derrick stated, "I really don't remember, but I can find out. I can ask Sheryl to check with the hotel. I see where you are going with this now!"

"Yeah, have her do that. Because if so. Whoever was in the room when Tay went in, could have come in by an adjoining room door. And that could also be how they escaped without anyone else seeing them."

Derrick immediately got up and got his phone. He tried to call Sheryl, but there was no answer. Then he called Keith and he picked right up. "Hey, Keith. Passion and I were having a conversation and she made a good point about something. We want to know if there was an adjoining door in the hotel room Tay and I were in. I tried to call Sheryl, but she didn't answer. Is there any way you can find out for me?"

"Yes, I can call the hotel myself. Great point too! If that is true. It may give some answers to a lot of the unanswered questions. Give me a minute and I will call you all right back." Keith said before hanging the phone up.

We were waiting anxiously for Keith to call us back. Sitting there Derrick and I continued to try to piece things together. It's amazing how we went from arguing to trying to solve the missing pieces from the incident. Then finally the phone rang. Derrick hurried up and answered it, but instead of it being Keith. It was Sheryl. Derrick advised her of what he called her for. He also explained to her that he was waiting on Keith to provide of return call regarding the adjoining doors. Sheryl told Derrick that she didn't even think about that. They kept talking about what he and I were discussing when Derrick told Sheryl Keith was calling in. He merged the calls and let Keith know Sheryl was on the line too. He had already put the call on speaker phone so I could hear what they were saying as well.

"Well, Derrick! Looks like Passion was right. There were adjoining doors in that room. The reason no one knew was because the adjoining door was inside of the closet. The hotel had remodeled some years back and made closets over the adjoining doors. That's not the only information I found out neither. Seems like that room was reserved at the same time the other room was, by the same person. So, Derrick. I must ask you. Who reserved the room?" Keith asked.

"Tay did!" Derrick answered.

"Ok, now we are really in a loop. We got to find out if someone was in the other room waiting on you all. Or if Tay had something else planned out. Derrick does Passion know everything now regarding Tay?" Keith asked as though he wanted to inquire about something else.

"Yes, she does." Derrick answered.

"Ok, Sheryl since you are back home. Have someone find out the where about of Tayneshia's husband Mark that day. And see where his head is on everything. We just never know. He could have been watching her moves and knew about her getting the two rooms. Who knows? She could have plotted with him on some other shit, and he turned on her. Derrick, boy your ass has gotten in some real shit this time." Keith stated.

"Yes, he has!" Sheryl agreed.

Derrick just shook his head as though he agreed with them. I didn't say anything. I sat quietly like a little church house mouse. Keith and Sheryl went back and forth on their next steps to get things resolved, while we listened. They finally had their plans worked out and advised us that they would keep us updated. Sheryl advised us to hold on, and to try and enjoy the time we have in the Bahamas. She went on to tell us she would have us home real soon now that they see a break in the case. Funny thing is it took the very person they tried keeping in the dark to give them the clue they needed. But for me, I still believe they are barking up the wrong tree. My woman's intuition is telling me Mark had nothing to do with this. I really believe Candice is behind the whole thing and she used Stephanie as a pond. Sheryl and Keith can chase after Mark and his where about, but I'm going to do a little investigation myself on them two heifers. And I know exactly who to reach out to. See, Marlon gave me some information I could use to black mail a little birdie at the office. I'm sure she doesn't want Daddy to know his daughter had a threesome with one of his paralegals and her husband. That wouldn't look good around the office and sure wouldn't look good for her as well. Especially, since her husband is the top lawyer at the firm. Sheryl and Keith disconnected the call while Derick and I sat there looking at each other.

"Well, Babe. Looks like we might be going home soon." Derrick stated.

"I wouldn't count your chickens before they hatch! I really don't think Mark had anything to do with it. I'm going to put my money on Candice." I reiterated to him.

"Why are you so set on Candice? I know she is evil, but I don't think she is that crazy to try and kill me."

"And why don't you believe she wouldn't? Are you not telling me something about you and Candice?" I asked.

"No! I've told you everything. It's just Candice has always played tough, but she soft as cotton candy. Her ass wouldn't shoot a thing." Derrick said with a straight face.

"Well, you believe that, but I sure don't." I said getting up to go to the restroom.

"Where are you going?" He asked.

"Can a girl use the restroom?" I said continuing to my destination.

As soon as I got in the bathroom, I sent Marlon a message to let him know I needed to see him later somehow. He quickly responded back and stated get away and come to my room. After receiving his message. I sat in the bathroom trying to come up with a plan of escape. But I was unable to think of one currently. Therefore, I finished up in the bathroom and went back into the living area. Derrick had turned on the TV and was now watching the local news. The weatherman was on the screen showing a forecast for some thunderstorms that could be hitting within the next hour. There it was. I could maybe escape once the thunderstorms hit if Derrick would fall asleep. The rain and thunder seemed to always make him sleepy. Hopefully, the storm would move in quickly and he would do as usual. Because that would be the only way I could escape. I really need to see Marlon in person to see if he knows all the information I have just learned.

"Passion looks like a storm is coming. We will need to try tomorrow to go where I wanted to take you. Unless you don't mind trampling in the water?" Derrick asked.

"No, I don't want to get all wet. I'm ok with staying in. I need to try and call Mr. Davis since we don't know how long we will be gone."

"That's ok P! I told you. Sheryl would tell the people who needed to know where we are. Mr. Davis was one of them. He also knows not to tell anyone at the office. Mr. Davis told Sheryl to tell you not to worry about work. He would see you when you get back. He just wants us to be safe." Derrick explained.

"Really! The more I try to get over new information. You spring more on me. I just don't understand why I have to be kept in the dark about so much stuff!" I said slamming the glass of water down on the coffee table.

"Passion, I'm sorry babe! Damn! I'm going to just shut my mouth for a while. Every time I say something, you get an attitude. I can't stress it enough. I'm just trying to make sure we are ok! I'm going in the bedroom and take a nap. Hopefully by the time I get up. The storm will have come and gone. Then maybe we can get out this room and go have some fun. I see all that has happened is getting to the both of us." He said getting up and walking into the bedroom.

After getting into the bedroom, Derrick closed the door. This made me think he didn't want any company. So, I continued sitting on the couch watching the news. Looks like, I won't have to wait long before I can escape off to Marlon's room after all. The opportunity I needed had just presented itself by Derrick taking a nap. I waited a while until I heard Derrick snoring and I made my escape.

CHAPTER

14

Easing out of the door was simple because Derrick had closed the bedroom door. Therefore, it would block out some of the noise of me shutting the front door. I gently shut the door and dashed to Marlon's room. I gave him a call on my way to let him know I was in route. Marlon was already at the door waiting when I made it there.

"Passion, what's going on now that it is urgent you see me?" Marlon asked.

"Marlon, I need to ask you a question and you need to be honest with me. Did you know that Tayneshia's Son was Derrick's?"

"P, you are playing right? Hell no! I did not know that. Derrick sure did keep that a secret. Where did you find that information out at?" He asked.

"He told me today! Supposedly, the child became sick and needed some blood. Tay's husband tried donating and found out he wasn't the father. She contacted Derrick and he got tested. That's when they found out the child was his. Oh! You have not heard the best of it. He found out about his HIV status then too!" I said slanting my head to the side.

"Wait! Wait, Passion! He knew before you all went to the doctor and never said shit to you? How long has he known?"

"He said about two months before the shooting. Evidently, Keith and Derrick had a talk about it today. Keith told him he needed to tell me everything before it comes out. So now they believe Mark has something to do with the shooting."

"Dang! This mess is way out there." Marlon said in disbelief.

Looking at Marlon. I could tell he didn't have a clue about this. "Marlon, let me give you the other news. I started thinking about the hotel room Derrick and Tay was at as well. So, I asked Derrick was there adjoining doors in the room. Come to find out there were. They were not in plain view because the hotel remodeled years ago and put the adjoining doors inside closets. Whoever did this could have already been in the room. Who's to say?"

Marlon escorted me over to sit down. We were still standing in front of the door while I gave him the tea.

"Babe, I must ask you now! Are you still going to stay trapped in that marriage after finding out more of his crap?"

"Marlon, Hell No! I'm so mad. I want to leave now, but we are over here. If we were back home. I would move all my stuff in an instance." I said as I started to cry.

"Who said you can't leave now? All you got to do is tell me you are ready to go. And I will make it so we can get out of here and no one will have to know." He said grabbing my left hand.

"How? Won't Keith know you're gone? Ever thought that he may tell Derrick about you being here too?" I asked.

"You let me handle that! I told you Keith and I have history. He might work with Sheryl, but I knew him back when he wasn't so squeaky clean. Why do you think he told me about you all coming over here, and then he helped me sneak over here? Keith knows how I feel about you. And let's just say I have more pull with him than Sheryl does. So, tell me right now, if you are ready to go, and I will get everything taking care of for us to leave?" He asked.

"Yes, I'm ready! But we can't go back to Tenison right now. Can we?"

"We don't have to. I have been setting up a resident in the north. I've been wanting to leave Texas for some time now." Marlon said in a convincing way.

"Marlon, I want too so bad. But you're scaring me too, with all the new secrets you are revealing right now. Are you sure we can trust Keith?"

Marlon looked at me gazing in my eyes and gripping my face with both his hands and said, "Passion, I promise, it will be ok. Give me a day or two. I'm going to get with Keith tonight and make plans. I will be in contact with you as soon as everything is ready. P, please don't be playing with me. I've been waiting on you to leave that bastard." Marlon said with a strong tone.

"You just get everything ready. I guess I can put up with him a little longer."

Marlon and I kissed erratically, until I pushed away. "Marlon, I got to get back before he wakes up."

"Ok, babe! Be careful and call me if you need me. And don't be having sex with him either." He said slapping me on my butt as I walked to the door.

"Shut up! I got this. "I said giving him another kiss on his lips.

Walking out of Marlon's room and hurrying back to our room. I noticed a woman walking down the hallway. She had a scarf covering her head with some dark shades on. She also had on a flower swimsuit and a pair of matching flip flops as though she was returning from the beach area. The lady carried a large bag with items inside of it. It looked like the items were things of use to maybe sit in the sun or go swimming. But unfortunately, because of the weather. It looks like her plans may have gotten rained out. As we passed each other, I could see her eyes slanting to the side to get a quick view of me. I turned my head to get a full view of her. Because as we got closer, I could see she was one of the bartenders who was working at the Junction the day I met Marlon. She did not speak to me and I surely didn't speak to her. All I wanted to do was get back inside the room before Derrick woke up. And after arriving at the room and getting inside. I had succeeded at it. He was still snoring loudly, and I could hear the thunderstorm roaring as well. I opened the bedroom door and made my way to my side of the bed. For Derrick not to smell any trace of Marlon's cologne on me. I pulled off my clothing and got in the bed with my birthday suit on. He was so relaxed that he did not move a muscle from me getting in the bed. Knowing that Marlon is working on an escape for us. It was easy for my mind to relax and I drifted fast to sleep.

Awakening and looking around the room, I noticed that Derrick was no longer in the bed with me. Sitting up. I called his name.

"Derrick!"

"Yes Passion. I'm in the kitchen." He replied.

After hearing his response. I decided to take a shower before joining him in the kitchen. The evening nap did do me some justice. But the thought of hot shower water hitting my body in the right spots, could relieve the rest of the tension in certain areas. Therefore, I picked up my clothes off the floor and proceeded into the bathroom. Since I was already in my birthday suit, I got in the shower. Twirling my body around in the water. I could feel my body relaxing, and the heat steaming from the water made different areas of my body become aroused. I turned my frontal area to the water and let it massage my private areas. My nipples were extremely hard, and my clitoris pulsated. I started to visualize Marlon in the shower with me. Massaging my own body parts. I reached my climax. Only if Marlon could have really been a part of this five-minute relief tactic. It would have given me more pleasure. Finishing up my shower. I removed myself from the shower area and freed myself from the wetness of the water. I slipped on a t-shirt dress and went into the kitchen to join Derrick. When I arrived. Derrick was cooking dinner.

"Looks like you enjoyed a good nap too." He stated.

"Yes! I did. Did I sleep that long? It looks like you went and made groceries?"

"Yes, you been sleep for about three hours. I didn't go and actually get them. I used a service they have over here that will deliver the groceries to you. Since the storm is continuing, I decided to cook us a late dinner."

Looking out the patio door, I could see it was still raining and nightfall had fell. Derrick made an excellent choice regarding ordering groceries and cooking in. This will allow us to stay dry and we will not have to move around in the storm. Sitting down at the dining room table and facing Derrick, reminded me of how great of a cook he is. He likes to event new meals using various food groups and ingredients. One could only imagine what our dinner will consist of tonight. From the aroma in the air. It smells like some Italian food. Sniffing in the air, I tried to guess exactly what it maybe.

"What are you cooking? It smells like some lasagna or spaghetti." I asked.

"Yes, it is Italian food, but not lasagna or spaghetti. I have some chicken parmesan smothered in tomato sauce cooking with melted mozzarella cheese. Along with that, I made a broccoli salad with vinaigrette dressing, and garlic bread. Also, I added a soft white wine to drink. I know how you don't care for spaghetti and don't like much alcohol. I wanted you to enjoy the meal since today has been unenjoyable for you."

"Ok, thanks for that Derrick. The meal sounds delicious and smells even better! "I stated waiting on him to complete the plates for dinner.

Derrick completed the dinner plates and placed them on the table. He poured the wine and sat down across from me. We prayed over the meal and we started to eat our dinner. In the middle of our dinner there was a knock at the door. Derrick looked at me and said, "I wonder who that could be!" He got up and went to answer the door. Looking through the peep hole he saw that it was Keith. Derrick opened the door and advised Keith to come on in. To my surprise Keith was accompanied with the female I saw in the hallway. Immediately, my heart started to race with excitement. I started to wonder if she would say anything about Marlon and I being at the restaurant together. I prayed she acted accordingly, and that she acts as though we have never saw one another. Walking back to the dinner table, Derrick introduced me to Keith and the lady who accompanied him. He didn't state her name. Therefore, Keith provided a name of Lynn. Being courteous Derrick invited them to join us for dinner. But they both denied and sat down in the living area.

"Derrick, I just came by to give you an update on our conversation earlier. I didn't want to talk over the phone. Therefore, I decided to come in person. I hope it is ok with you and Passion, that I brought my lady friend with me." Keith stated.

"That's fine! It's nice to meet you, Lynn. "Derrick said while taking a sip of wine.

"Nice to meet you all as well. Now, maybe that I know there is another lady on this trip. I could have some company to roam the city." Lynn stated with a smile on her face.

"Yes Ma'am! I could use another lady to chat with as well. Talking to my husband and staying cooped up in this room has its disadvantages. I look forward to some girl time." I responded.

"Well, there you have it! Let's do a girl's brunch tomorrow at 11am?" She asked.

"Sure, you have a date." I advised.

After we had confirmed our brunch for the next day. Keith started to talk about the information he had received. He advised that Sheryl had contacted Mark and he told her he was at work that day. Mark informed Sheryl that she could call his job and get his clock in and out time. He went on to say he was notified by an officer and his Human Resource Department about his wife's death. There is no way he could have shot anyone. Sheryl checked his alibi, and it was confirmed that Mark was at work. So, Mark is no longer a suspect. But what Sheryl did find out was Tayneshia did not come to the room in her own car. One of the housekeepers saw her being dropped off. She got out of a grey SUV of some sort. The housekeeper didn't know what kind of SUV it was. She only remembered the color. Also, she did say she got dropped off by another female. Therefore, we are looking into a female with a grey SUV that Tayneshia may know. "Derrick and Passion that leaves me to ask you all do y'all know of such lady?"

"I don't." Derrick responded.

"I'm not familiar with a grey SUV at the moment, but I can try and contact Tay's Mom and see if she can give me any information." I stated.

"Passion! See what you can find out and let me know." Keith said getting up off the couch. "Derrick, I'm sorry we interrupted you all's dinner. I just wanted to tell you all the information in person, and plus we were headed downstairs for dinner. We were going to invite you all, but you all are already eating. Therefore, we shall talk tomorrow."

"Ok Keith. Thanks so much!" Derrick said walking them to the door.

"Passion, please don't forget about brunch tomorrow. I will meet you at the restaurant at 11am. I can't wait to get to know you better." Lynn stated winking her eye at me as she went out the door.

Before I could respond. Derrick closed the door. He walked back to the dinner table with a peculiar look on his face. He looked as though he wasn't pleased with the information Keith had just provided. Derrick picked up his plate and proceeded to the trash can to dump the rest of his food. This made me think he was worried about something.

"Derrick are you ok? You didn't even complete the rest of your food." I asked.

"Yes babe. I'm okay. It just seems like every time I believe we are on the right track to who shot me. Things get kicked back to square one. I want to go home just like you P. But most of all, I want all this shit to be resolved and whoever to be held accountable for their actions. I know I've been an ass for years, but for that girl to lose her life and even for me to get shot. Isn't right!" He said hitting his fist on the counter.

I could tell he was feeling sorrowful and a part of me wanted to get up to console him. But the other part of me became angry. Was he crying out for Tayneshia now? Has whatever he felt for her started to eat at his conscious as well? Or was he really frustrated because someone finally outsmarted his actions of cheating? The rabbit that usually had the gun is now standing with the gun pointed at him. Funny thing is, he has no clue of who the rabbit is!

Thinking in my head about who the rabbit could be. I got up to clear my plate as well and finish cleaning up the kitchen with Derrick. We straightened things back up and went to enjoy the rest of the evening in the bedroom. Derrick took him a shower. I decided to search the internet on my laptop to occupy my time. Getting logged into my laptop seemed inedible. Especially, since the storm continued to rage outside. Finally, I was able to get in. I wanted to check my emails to see if Marlon had emailed any information. I had not heard from him. He had not made any kind of contact with me after we spoke earlier. Unfortunately, there was no email from Marlon, but there sure was one from the anonymous person.

Dear Passion,

It appears you and your cheating ass husband have disappeared from the face of the earth. Now, I know you're wondering. How does this person keep getting all my contact information? Well, darling! There is this thing called the World Wide Web. ☺ And plus, I needed to drop some more information on the perfect little wife who has decided to stay with her husband, after everything he has done. Don't you feel just a little angry about him cheating with your best friend, his best friend's wife, and his high school sweetheart? And who knows who else! Sorry to be the bearer of bad news, but a little birdie told me something else! Your cheating ass husband has a child you know nothing about. Ohhhhh! And I'm not talking about the dead child or Tay's child either. Oops! Are did you even know about Tay's child? This is what you call her isn't it? Well, Well! That's all for now. Girl, you better ask him about that baby. Because he or she hasn't even been born yet! ☺ ☺

Sayonara,
Your Secret Advisor!

Reading this email made steam start to form in my head. I felt like the bulls in a rodeo getting ready to attack the man with the flag. Derrick came out the bathroom and I couldn't take my eyes off him.

"Passion why in the hell are you looking at me like that?" He asked.

I couldn't say a word at this point. I just turned the laptop toward his way. He sat down on the bed and grabbed the laptop. As he read, I folded my arms and waited on his response. I dared myself that no tears would fall out of my eyes. The only thing that would fall out these eyes right now is, the meaning he will need to get of this marriage is so over.

"What do you have to say about that?" I asked.

"Passion, I don't have to say anything about that! I told you about Lenton and I don't have any clues about another baby. Whoever this is! Is trying to mess with your head. Matter of fact, we need to get Sheryl them to investigate your email address. This person could have connection to the shooting. They sure seem to know a lot about me. And it also seems like they are watching us to know we are not around. You haven't been responding to this person, have you? "Derrick asked.

"Hell no! This is the first time they have emailed my personal email. They contacted me on my work email before. Sad to say, the other information they sent was correct about you and Stephanie. So, why shouldn't I believe there is another baby?"

"Believe what you want! At this point, I'm so fucking tired of you believing everybody else. I do not care. I said there is no other baby to my knowledge! I know what I'm about to do is call Sheryl. We are going home tomorrow or the next day. I'm going to let her know, I want to come home ASAP. I'm not running from anyone no more. Yes, I have done dirt and many others have as well. Leaving my life behind and running from whoever this coward is, won't be my lifestyle. So, Passion you can keep entertaining these fools. I have asked God to forgive me and that is all I need. I have asked you repeatedly and if you don't want to. Then maybe you are right. We need to divorce!" He said giving the laptop back and walking out the room.

Watching Derrick walk out the room and meditating on what he stated. Put me in a vulnerable state. I started to think what if he is right. This person could be involved and messing with my head. But I really can't afford to think about the anonymous caller at this point. I must shift my focus in another direction because Derrick is making plans to go home soon. While Marlon is making other plans for us as well. I got to make my mind up on who I want to leave with. Here I am again trapped on trying to make the right decision in my relationships.

CHAPTER

15

L ast night was the longest night I had experienced in a while. Derrick slept in the living room and I remained in the bedroom. We didn't talk to one another after he stated that we may need a divorce. I didn't get much sleep at all. I kept thinking about what decision would best benefit me. I tried to weigh the pros and cons of leaving Derrick and going with Marlon. Then on the other hand. I had to weight the same pros and cons of going with Marlon and leaving Derrick. The biggest pro or con right now, happens to be the question that is ringing in my head. Is the information true about another baby, or is it all made up information to get me off track? If I could just find out the truth about it. I may be able to decide without any regrets.

Sitting here thinking. I heard voices in the living room. I wasn't sure if Derrick was on the phone, or actually there was someone else in there with him. Therefore, I walked to the bedroom door and looked into the living room. He was on the phone. He was talking with Sheryl. Derrick turned and saw me standing in the door and told me to come there for a minute. So, I proceeded to the living room and sat down beside him.

"Sheryl, Passion had just come in the room. Please tell her what you have found out about those emails everyone is getting." He said looking directly in my face.

"Good Morning Passion! Derrick told me about the email you got. I took the liberty and had some back-end work done on emails being submitted to your email address. See, what people don't understand just because they try and block their email name. We can still get access to their server, email link, and phone numbers. You will never guess who has been sending you emails?" Sheryl stated.

"Hey Sheryl. Please oblige me!"

Sheryl took a deep breath and spoke out in a sigh of relief, "It is Janelle. Tay's sister. Looks like she owns a gray Tahoe too! I've tried calling her as well but have been unsuccessful. I didn't want to bother them too much right now, since the funeral is this weekend. I have already told Derrick as soon as the funeral is over. We will be sending someone out to bring her in to discuss her whereabouts that day and to discuss the emails."

"Sounds good Sheryl. I understand it could be Janelle with the emails, but what would be her reason to shoot Tay and Derrick?"

"Well, I'm glad you asked Passion. I do not think she shot them. I believe she may have information that can help us find who wanted to. I also, believe she called you to see what you knew and how you were feeling about everything. Therefore, checking on you may have got her more information. But because you had an attitude it did not work. So, I told Derrick you all can come home tomorrow. I have a strong feeling of who all is involved, and we can issue warrants to bring them in. I just need to speak with Janelle to confirm somethings. So, you all go ahead and get packed. I will get you all's departure information together. Oh! I already told Derrick, please do not reach out to anyone. We've got to make sure you all are safe. Derrick, I will send you the flight information in a little bit. I must go now. I have a meeting in about twenty minutes. Please do not worry Passion. I got it under control. Love you both. Talk to you all later!" Sheryl said as she hung up the phone.

Sitting in disbelief, Derrick and I sat in quietness for a minute. All I could wonder about was how is Janelle involved and why? Who else is Sheryl talking about?

"P, I guess we better talk about what is going to happen when we get home. I want this marriage to work, but after reviewing my mistakes. I do not see how. I blame myself for all of this. Babe, I cannot turn back the hands of time, but I can promise you to go forward I am going to do better. Passion, I am human, and I will still make mistakes! But will you be able to deal with everything?" Derrick said crying.

"Derrick, we have both made mistakes. Yes, you've caused a lot of this. But I am to blame as well. I knew you were continuously cheating, and I put up with it. So, I must point some fingers at myself too. To be honest with you Derrick. I cannot do this anymore. And if there is another baby coming. I sure cannot handle that! When we get back home. I am going to get my things and just leave. I hope you really understand!" I said standing up to go back into the bedroom.

Derrick stood up as well. He was trying to use his body as a blocking mechanism to keep me from leaving. Unfortunately, it did not work, because I moved him a side with a quick push. I proceeded to go to get dress to meet Lynn for our scheduled brunch. At this point I really needed a girl's talk. I do not know much about Lynn, but the vibe I got from her was pretty much okay.

As I got dressed. I sent Marlon a message to let him know of the conversation we had with Sheryl. I also informed him that we would be leaving tomorrow. I advised him that I was going to face the music back home and leave Derrick. I apologized if he had already made plans for us to escape, but the only way we all could start to live our lives is to face everything. With crazy thoughts flowing through my mind, I completed getting dress and left the room. I was still harboring the pain of hearing about another baby that; I did not even say goodbye to Derrick. I just went straight out of the door and headed to the restaurant. Once I reach the restaurant. I saw Lynn sitting at a table in the corner. I walked over and greeted Lynn with a friendly hug before sitting adjacent of her.

"Hello Passion! How are you today? I just love that sundress." She stated.

"I'm ok. I guess! It has been a long night and an even longer morning. Sorry, for bring my bad energy, but this is a much-needed girl's time. Lynn, please forgive me for my rudeness. Thanks for the compliment. I like your sundress as well. It goes well with your eye color."

Lynn was a middle-aged woman who has taken great care of her skin and body. She is the true meaning of black does not crack. She has an athletic body and no wrinkles in sight. Lynn has blonde tinted hair with hazel eyes. You can tell she also visits a manicurist often because her nails and toes were well-manicured. Lynn's sundress has a mixture of colors of orange, brown, yellow, and white. Which brought out her eye color. The design of the dress was stunning. It wrapped around her neck, and it drooped down her back which showed off her physique. She reminded me of the Angela Bassett type.

"Thanks Passion! I ordered us two Long Islands Teas to drink. I hope it is not too early for you. I also went ahead and ordered us bacon, eggs, toast, and some tropical fruit. Is that ok with you?" She asked.

"Thanks! You and I are going to get a long really well. Magnificent choices with it all. And yes, I need the long islands tea! Maybe it will calm some of these nerves that are running rapidly inside me." I said giving Lynn a big smile.

"Well, good! So how are you enjoying the Bahamas? I love it! I was glad when Keith asked me to tag a long."

"It is a beautiful place, but I haven't enjoyed it much at all. I am not sure if Keith has explained to you why we are here. I thought coming here would bring about different results, but it has only brought more horror."

"Yes, Keith did explain what is going on with you and your husband. Passion, I must be honest. I know about what is going on with you and Marlon too. Wait before you respond! Being a woman who has been through what you are going through right now. I dare not pass judgement on you. But what I will say is, be careful. And I'm not saying be careful about the men. I am saying be careful about you. Let me share something with you if that is ok with you?" Lynn asked.

"Why sure! Go ahead. I told you. I needed this girl talk. I'm all ears." I said as I sat closer to the table.

"Okay. I know you may be wondering what kind of relationship Keith and I have. Well, I met Keith through my ex-husband years ago. My ex-husband was a cheater as well. You name it. He did it. He messed with all types of women and had outside children as well. But he and I never had children. He blamed me for his cheating. Hell, I blamed me for his cheating. I went through depression. Had weight problems. Lost friends and felt worthless. Babe, I even tried to kill myself. But God sent Keith to be my strong tower during it all. He was a great friend who later became a lover. I felt bad about messing around with him at first. But it was an older lady who told me. Do not overlook your blessing by listening to what other's may say is not right. I took her advice. Keith and I have not got married, but we have a wonderful relationship. He understands me and I understand him. I know you remember me from the Junction Restaurant. I could see it all in your face. Especially, when we passed each other in the hallway yesterday. And when I came into the room yesterday evening. I saw how your face dropped wondering what I might say. That is why I had the biggest grin on my face. I told Keith when we left that you were so afraid." She stated as she let out a giggle.

"Yes Ma'am. I was terrified." I said while laughing.

Listening to Lynn share her story put me at ease with her. It reminded me of how Tay and I use to share stories. We would cry, laugh, and get mad all at the same time. It sure felt good to be in the presence of another woman who understood what I am going through. Lynn gave off an energy that only God could provide. Her spirit kind of reminded me of my Mom. At this stage of my life. I needed a mother figure, and Lynn just might be the replacement that God has sent.

"So, tell me how are you feeling? I've heard Keith talk about Marlon's and Derrick's feelings. But he has never mention anything about yours." She replied.

"Ms. Lynn too be honest with you. I don't know how I feel. Some days I am ok. Then other days I am numb. I keep telling myself I love my husband, but then I tell myself I love Marlon. The more things come out. I hate Derrick and everything he stands for. All I think about now is getting even. Thinking this way, brings me to wonder if I really love Derrick like I say I do. I'm so confused at times. And I can't lie. Sometimes I wish I would have been the one that pulled the trigger on them." I stated as tears came into play in my eyes.

"Passion, I totally understand. Been there and done that! Remember I told you earlier to be careful of you."

"Yes Ma'am. I remember."

"What I meant by that was, don't get caught up in trying to prove to either man your love for him. That will cause you to forget to love yourself first. Yes, Derrick is your husband, and you may love him. But never let him use that love against you. And the same for Marlon. See as women we love so hard, that we will make sure they are good, before we make sure we are. Sometimes we do this without even knowing it. For me just listening to Keith. Marlon fell in love with you because

Derrick left him doing his husband duties, and then he could not keep his feelings under control. As for Derrick, he loves you too, but need other women to validate whatever he feels he is not getting from you. When all he really had to do was communicate that with you so you both could work through the issues. And now that the women who validated those issues may be gone or leaving. He wants to remain with what he does get at home rather than to have nothing. Passion all I'm trying to say is, sweetheart get back to loving yourself. And if the love you have for yourself includes Derrick or Marlon. Please make sure they will put you first. I can see it all in your face that you love them both. I can also see you love your husband more than you love Marlon. You are kind of just like Derrick. You are so afraid of losing what may be your good thing. That you're at in a place of uncertainty. You do not know if it is Derrick or Marlon. Am I correct?" Lynn asked.

Nodding my head in agreement with Lynn, I noticed Marlon walking in the restaurant. He walked in looking around as if he was making sure Derrick was not around. He came over to the table and greeted us both.

"Good Afternoon Ladies. I hope you all are enjoying yourself." He said in a nice way. "Passion, I got your text and came to let you know I am leaving now. Derrick messaged me this morning letting me know you all where here in the Bahamas and why. He apologized for all that has happened between us and wants to move forward. He let me know that he understood things may not be the same, but he would like to remain friends. He said yawl would be returning tomorrow and he needed me to pick you all up from the airport. I didn't want to make him suspicious of anything, so I agreed. What really freaked me out was, he said he knew I loved you. He even stated he would step out of the way for your happiness. I am not sure why he said all of that. So, I did not question him at that point. I'm sure you will be ok now that you have met Ms. Lynn. She is a phenomenal woman and will make sure you are ok. Oh yeah! Ms. Lynn. I have spoken with Keith and he let me know, that you all will be coming back with them. Therefore, I will meet you all at the airport. Lynn, please keep an eye on her for me. If you do not mind?" Marlon said smiling.

"You got it Marlon!" Lynn responded.

Standing up to give Marlon a hug. I let him know I would be okay, and we would talk as soon as I got home. He gave Lynn a hug and left the restaurant. Lynn and I finished our meal and got to know each other better. My intuition was right about her. She had experience many of life's hardships and overcome them. She reminded me of how as people we should share our testimonies. We never know who it might encourage or heal. Because whether she knows it or not, her testimony today has given me the power to walk away from my marriage and embrace the real love I have been missing. And that would be loving myself first. I don't know if Marlon will be the next true love. What I do know is my happiness won't be trapped in another man, but in the man above.

"Lynn, I have to say thank you for inviting me to this brunch. It gave me so much hope. Please, let's stay in contact! I have no real friends left and would love for you to be a new one." I said giving her another hug.

"Sure honey! I could use a good friend as well. And it was my pleasure to bring you some comfort. That little birdie that just left felt like you needed to hear my testimony. And he was right. Now this old lady can't tell you what to do, but I wouldn't count him out if I was you. He is special. There is a lot you don't know about him as well. But that is not my place to tell you. Just keep that in mind." Lynn said as we walked out of the restaurant together.

Lynn and I continued our conversation about Marlon as we walked back to our hotel rooms. Talking with her brought about so much comfort in my heart, that I couldn't help but praise the Lord for sending her at the right time. And what she did as we prepared to depart from each other made me more thankful. She took a crystal angel out of her purse and placed it in my hand. She gave me specific instructions of what to do with it when I feel all alone. Lynn advised me that the same instructions were given to her and it helped her make it through. And she promised to pass it along to another deserving woman. Which just happened to be me. I accepted it with honor.

Holding my hands after she gave me the angel, Lynn started to pray.

"Father that is in heaven and also present on earth. I stand here today holding this young lady's hand to offer her up to you. She has been broken in so many ways. Therefore, I intercede on her behalf, and ask you to put her back together again. Allow her to have true loves and real friendships in her life. Don't allow her to remain trapped in anything that won't allow her to be what you have called her to be. God let her move forward in life being happier than before. Put the right people in place to assist her on her life's journey. This is my prayer to you for her! In Jesus Name, Amen!"

With tears in our eyes and embracing through our spiritual bond. Lynn and I finally departed. God had just reassured me he was present with me, and that he would use the right people to help me stay sane through it all. I must believe in him, and trust that he will do it.

CHAPTER

16

Upon returning to the hotel room, I began to dread going inside. After I made it back, I found Derrick laying on the sofa watching TV. The closer I got to his presence. I clutched the angel tighter. I was still carrying it in my hand. The room's atmosphere was still filled with the negative energy from the last couple of days. After having a wonderful morning with Lynn. I refused to let everything that happened between Derrick and I return me to a state of entrapment. I will no longer allow him or no one else to make me feel trapped by any means necessary. Funny thing is, the more I closed my hands to secure the angel. The more strength I felt in my spirit. I can agree with Lynn now, that the angel does bring about strength. Especially, when you know you are in a room with someone who can make you feel like you are presently in hell.

"Passion, did you enjoy your girl's brunch?" Derrick asked.

"Yes, I did! Lynn is a wonderful lady. I could use someone like her in my life." I stated walking closer to him.

"Well, that is good. Sheryl said she reminds her a lot of you, and she figured you all would get along great. I see she was right. Oh, before we get into any far-out conversations. I want to apologize for the things I said last night. While you were gone, I talked with Sheryl and she told me I was wrong. She made me see things from your point of view. And I want us to be on the same page about our marriage before we get back home. Sheryl booked our flights. We will be leaving incredibly early in the morning. I hope you do not mind that I took the liberty of contacting Marlon and asking him to pick us up from the airport. I needed someone trustworthy. Even after all that has occurred between us. I still feel he is." He said sitting up on the sofa.

"If you are fine with it. Then I am. I was under the impression he didn't want to see any of us, the way he stormed out of the house that day. But I am glad you all talked and agreed to work things out." I stated.

"Yes, me too Passion. I also wanted to let you know, because I did tell him that if you all wanted to be together. I'm ok with that too. I know he loves you and I feel you love him too. It is my fault that our marriage is in shambles not yawls'. Whether you believe me or not. I want you to be happy even if it means without me. Plus, I maybe dead soon anyways." Derrick stated with a nonchalant face.

"Derrick, I thank you for saying that, but why would you say, you will be dead soon? Where is all that faith you had a couple of days ago?" I asked sitting down next to him.

"Babe look at me and my situation. I caused someone to lose their life. Shit, I got a child thirteen years old and I haven't even been in their life. I have repeatedly hurt you and to top it all off. I contracted a disease that could kill me and if it does not. Whoever is after me may. I'm trying to have faith, but Passion all I have done. God maybe punishing me for it all!" He said as he leaned over in my lap.

Rubbing Derrick across his shoulders. I started to think about what he just stated. Ironically, on the TV was a commercial in which the devil was sitting on a man's left shoulder and an angel on his right shoulder. The devil was trying to get him to do evil, while the angel was trying to stop him. And here I was wanting to act just like a devil with my thoughts about Derrick's feelings, but my actions were showing my angel side. Continuing to hold the angel Lynn gave me in my left hand. I placed it in Derrick's hand. I wanted to transfer the strength that I experience from the angel into him.

Derrick looked at me and asked," Where did you get this?"

"Lynn gave it to me." The way he was looking at the angel was a look of familiarity. Derrick gave me the feeling that he had saw this angel before. So, I could not help but ask him. "Have you saw this before?"

"Yes, but I can't remember exactly were. Touching it gave me cold chills. I even had a vision of a little old lady." He answered staring at the angel.

"Lynn told me a little old lady gave it to her years ago. That's strange that you saw the little old lady by just a simple touch. Well since this is officially our last day in the Bahamas. What are we going to do?"

"You want to do something with me?" He asked surprised.

"Derrick, we might as well make the best of the time we have left here. I am not sure how you feel about going home, but I know somethings may be unpleasant. Therefore, I would like to have some fun memories to hold on to from the Bahamas. I don't want to only remember it as the place we ran to as an escape goat."

"Correct Passion. I feel you on that. Well, let me get dress, and then we can go where I wanted to care you last night."

After Derrick got dressed. He took me to an elegant nightclub. It was unlike any nightclub I had gone to before. A portion of the nightclub was inside, and the other portion was outside. There were two bars for drinks. One was inside, and the other one was outside in the middle of a swimming pool. There was different section to be seated and everything seemed to be made of glass. What really got my attention was the seating area also located in the swimming pool. Being fascinated by that. I asked Derrick if we could be seated in the pool area. He laughed and grabbed my hand to escort me outside.

Waiting to be seated Derrick and I enjoyed the breeze that blew across our faces. Looking around and enjoying the view I spotted a specific booth I wanted to be seated at. After showing Derrick the area. He agreed and made sure the waiter knew we were interested in being seated there. Finally, the waiter took us to that specific booth. It was so much fun walking through the water between tables and other people. Derrick held onto me in order to assist me with keeping my balance in the water. Arriving at our booth, I was expecting Derrick to sit across from me, but he sat on the same side as I was seated. Now our view consisted of the ocean, white doves, and everything else behind us. Oh, how I wished this were our life forever.

"Passion, why are you crying?" Derrick asked.

I didn't even realize that I had started to cry. This was such a wonderful view and I wanted it to be my life. Unfortunately, it could only be a wishful thought.

"Babe, I did not know the tears were coming down. I was thinking what if this was our lives right now. We could move forward and leave everyone and everything behind us. What if the shooting never happened? Also, what if you hadn't' cheated and I never cheated? We would still have our friendships. We would not be trapped in so much pain, hurt, envy, jealousy, and strife. Derrick, why! Why did you do this to us?

"Passion, I can't explain why. Once I started. I could not stop. I was like a crack head needing a fix! After a while, it became easy. The women were easy. But babe believe me! My love for you never changed. Passion! Answer this one question for me. Do you still love me?" Derick asked holding my hand.

Looking off before I answered his question. I replied," Yes, I still love you very much!"

"Well, if that is so. Let us make your thoughts our reality." He stated putting his hand on my face.

The crazy thing about Derrick's response was, which thought was he wanting to make our reality. Is it the thought of moving forward leaving everyone and everything behind? Surely, it's not the thought of our old friendships because some of them are unrepairable. How can I help him make my thoughts realities, when I'm unsure of which thought he is speaking about?

"Derrick exactly what do you mean?" I asked.

Gazing heavily into my eyes. Derrick spoke softly and said," I meant, let's start over right here! Right now! Let's leave everything and everyone behind. You said you love me, and I know I love you! Why go back to living in hell? Babe! Look at those waves! Can't you see us riding them? What about this gentle breeze being a constant reminder of fresh air? All you have to do is say yes, and I will call Sheryl right now and tell her we are not coming back. The Bahamas can become home. This can be our reality. What do you think P? Don't you want to live happily ever after?

I started to laugh at what Derrick had just said. Happily, ever after! I think not. How could we ever live that way? There are too many emotions and regrets still living inside of the both of us. We may cover them up, but we will never really get passed them. I couldn't even give him a straight answer at this point. To be honest, all I really wanted to do was to enjoy the rest of the afternoon.

"Passion, did you hear what I just ask you?" He asked.

"Yes Derrick. I heard you. That does sound nice and all. But I can't see me living over here forever. I remember you telling Sheryl you wanted to come home to face everything. You are correct! No more running. The only way to really tell if this marriage can be rebuilt. Is to go back to where it was torn down. Can't you see everything over here is easy for us now, because what causes us trouble isn't here. The real questions can only be answered when we are facing the problems." I explained.

"Okay. I totally understand. Please answer this question for me? When we get home, are we going to try to rebuild this marriage?" Derrick asked.

"I am not sure. We will just have to wait and see. But can you answer one question for me?" I asked looking at a message on my phone.

"And what might that question be?"

"Is Stephanie pregnant by you or Marlon?"

"What did you just say?" Derrick asked.

I leaned my phone over so Derrick could view the message I had just received. The evening was just spoiled. All of the beautification surrounding us right now, had turned very ugly in my view. I could no longer admire the view. All I saw was red staring at Derrick as he read the message. The message came from Stephanie's phone number. She wanted to let me know that she was pregnant. Stephanie went on to say in the message that, she was unsure of whom could be the father. She also advised me that she and Derrick lied about being involved with one another.

"Passion I just don't understand why everyone is seeking out to destroy us!" Derrick spoke in a loud voice.

"Really Derrick! Everyone is seeking to destroy us. No Sir! You destroyed us when you decided to step outside of the home for your pleasures. Wow! Just when I think we can make it in this marriage. Another blow hits me in my face. So, the email I received was right after all. There is another child." I responded with aggravation.

"I really don't think that is my child Passion. Think about it! If Stephanie got tested and she is negative. Then how could she have gotten pregnant by me. And plus, when I did have intercourse with her.

I used protection. I'm not going to believe that is my child until a blood test is performed." Derrick said as he gave me my phone back.

Sitting quietly for a moment, the thought of Marlon knowing crossed my mind. Is he aware of this new information? Did she message him as well? Will this change his view of his marriage? And will he still have the desires to move forward with me? This really puts a damper on both relationships I share with Derrick and Marlon. I sure could use another girl chat with Lynn at this point. Because right now, I really could walk out in the ocean and let the waves carry me away. But the real question is, who is the person behind the emails? They sure seem to know a lot about everyone involved, but we sure don't know anything about who they are.

"Well Derrick. I guess you are right. We do have to wait for a blood test, but it sure seems like Stephanie is pointing the finger at you. Because why would she want me to know she could be pregnant by you?" I asked.

"I don't know, but I am almost positive. I am not the father." Derrick stated as he looked over the menu. "Passion lets just order some food and try to enjoy the rest of the evening."

Agreeing with him, I started to review the menu. After deciding upon a meal, Derrick and I ordered our food. We had dinner and tried to talk about other things besides the text message. Finishing up dinner, Derrick asked if there was anything else I would like to see before returning to the room. Unfortunately, there was not anything that came to my mind. Therefore, I advised him that we could just walk around the area and sight see. He agreed and we left the club.

Derrick and I decided to go to the beachfront to stroll along the waters. Walking along the shores sure brought about a great peace. We both needed some peace at this point. Since our clothing was already wet from the club. I asked Derrick if we could walk in the water a little. Kicking my feet in the water, reminded me of how I use to play in the rain when I was a little girl. I would wait until the rain poured down before asking my Mom's permission to go out in it. Once I arrived in the downpour of the rain. I embraced the raindrops touch. It was a touch that I couldn't describe, but its touch felt wonderful. And right now, the touch of the water from the ocean felt the same way. I felt a sense of healing elevating through my body as we walked. Wondering if Derrick was feeling the same, I turned to ask him.

"Derrick, does the water against your feet have a gentle touch? It sure does for mine."

"Passion I was just about to ask you the same question. I feel a sense of peace, and I even felt a tingling sensation within. I wonder what that is all about? It kind of feels like the feelings one gets, when he first acknowledges his love for Christ." Derrick stated.

"Yes, it does! I didn't think about it in that way." I said as I stopped in my tracks.

Looking ahead of us, I thought I saw a woman who looked just like Candice. I shook my head and tried to focus my eyes for the long view. Still unsure. I asked Derrick to look ahead.

"Babe, look down there! Doesn't that lady look like Candice to you?"

"Where? I see several ladies ahead of us?" He asked.

"Derrick, look straight ahead to the left of the other ladies. There is a woman in a white swimsuit squatting playing in the water."

"Yes, I see her now. That is Candice! What in the hell is she doing over here?" Derrick said angrily. "Let's go back to the hotel. If she hasn't spotted us by now. I sure don't want her to."

We turned around and headed back to the hotel. Once we arrived at the entrance of the hotel, I turned around to see if she had followed us back. Unfortunately, she was nowhere in sight. Derrick and I walked swiftly down the hallway. It was like we were racing each other to the room. Once inside, Derrick went from room to room as though he was checking to make sure everything was ok. I sat at the dining room table watching him.

"Why do you think she is here? Could someone have alerted her of our whereabouts?" I asked Derrick.

"I'm not sure Passion. I'm fixing to call Keith and let him know. Give me one moment." He said while sitting down at the table too.

Picking up his phone, Derrick dialed Keith's number. "Hello Keith. I hate to bother you this evening, but we spotted Candice on the beach. I'm not sure if she saw us, but I want to be cautious. Especially, since we don't know if she is a part of any of this."

"Did you say Candice is over here? How the hell did she know you all was here?" Keith said eagerly.

"I'm not sure Keith. Passion and I will stay inside, until we leave in the morning. Hopefully, she is here on a vacation and not to make trouble. But we can't take any chances." Derrick stated.

"Exactly! You all sit tight, and we will roam around and see what we can find out. She doesn't know anything about Lynn and I. Maybe, Lynn can cross her path and get some information for us. As soon as I know something I will let you all know."

"Ok Keith. That's sounds great! Be careful though. Candice is not the average woman. She stays ready."

"Well, Derrick. I think Lynn is a perfect match for her. She stays ready as well." Keith said chuckling.

Saying goodbye. Derrick hung up the phone. We continued to sit at the dining table. Our conversation moved from trying to figure out why Candice may be here, to what we could do for the rest of the evening. Unsure of what to do. We decided to place spades. Derrick remembered that he packed the cards in our bags before we left home. Playing spades has always been a fun game to play in our families. I was taught at an early age how to play spades and after I met Derrick, he taught me some new techniques to the game too. We would often be partners at family events. Because of our winning streaks. People would always say we were cheating. But in reality, Derrick and I studied each other's playing strategies. Therefore, if I played certain cards. He knew what I had in my hand, and he knew exactly what cards to play. Playing cards tonight against one another could be interesting. Because playing each other and knowing each other's strategies, may make the game to harder for anyone of us to win. Looks like, we are going to have to change up our personal strategy to win against each other. Funny thing is, thinking back over our marriage. Derrick and I have been playing spades in it as well. We started out knowing the strategy of our marriage and we were winning. But as soon as Derrick started cheating with the other women. He messed up our partnership and we started to lose the game of marriage spades. He left me to learn new strategies which caused me to seek a new partner outside of our marriage. Now look at us. Instead of us winning the game of marriage spades. We are losing.

"Passion, looks like I win again!" Derrick said sarcastically.

"Yes, I guess you do." I said jokingly. "Well Derrick. I'm done for tonight. I'm going to go take a shower and get ready for bed since we are leaving so early in the morning."

"Okay. I am going to stay up for a while. I want to wait on Keith to call back. You can go ahead." He responded.

Getting up and going into the bedroom to prepare for my shower, my mind was set on messaging Marlon about Candice. Once I was secure in the bathroom. I contacted Marlon. He quickly responded. His message was that of disbelief. He was just like us. He couldn't understand why she was over here as well. Marlon advised me to be safe and not to worry, because Keith and Lynn were still here with us too. But, just to see those word in the message wasn't enough assurance for me. So, I tiptoed to the bedroom door and peeped to make sure Derrick was occupied. Therefore, I could call Marlon. Spying on Derrick for just a few seconds made me become more fearful. I found him pacing back in forth in the living room talking on his phone. Whoever he was talking to sure wasn't Keith. I heard Derrick say, "You are going to mess up everything for me. Why are you doing this." With a blank stare, I started to wonder if he was speaking with Candice. Just as I tried to hear more, Derrick looked towards the bedroom door. I quickly ran back into the bathroom and got back in the shower. After I heard him enter the bedroom, I turned off the shower to keep him from coming in and seeing the droplets of water on the floor from my feet. He quickly went back into the other room. Therefore, I got out of the shower and locked the bathroom door. In order for Derrick not to hear me talking. I turned the shower back on. Then I proceeded to call Marlon.

"Marlon are you busy?" I asked.

"No Passion. What's up?" Marlon asked.

"I am so afraid. I just overheard Derrick telling someone on the phone that they are going to mess up everything for him. I don't know if he was talking to Candice or not. I had to run back in the bathroom before he discovered I was listening. Marlon, I hate you left." I said frantically.

"Passion, calm down! Keith and Lynn are working on finding out something right now. I just talked to him. I'm sure everything will be ok. And I am sorry I left too. Truth be told, I miss you." He stated sadly.

"And another thing. Stephanie messaged me earlier and said she is pregnant. Are you aware of that?" I asked.

"Yes I am. But I am not convinced about that. Stephanie cannot have any more children. Something happened to her body when she was pregnant with our daughter that prevents her from having one. She is now trying to say it must have corrected itself. Passion every time I say I want a divorce, or I'm leaving. She pulls this stunt. So don't believe that mess. And if she is. I will be getting a blood test to make sure I am the father. If the child turns out to be mine. I will take it too. Please stop all the worrying. You will be home tomorrow, and we will work on you getting away from Derrick. Is that still the plan?" Marlon stated.

"Yes, so please be ready. Thanks for putting my fears at ease. I'm going to get off the phone now. I think I hear him coming in the bedroom."

"Okay, Goodnight! I love you Passion." He spoke.

Marlon always says I love you when we depart from one another. Because I am unsure of my feelings. I don't ever state it back to him. I don't want to lead him on in anyway. But I can tell myself, that I really do love him. I just don't love him more than I love Derrick.

"Passion are you finished?" Derrick asked.

"Yes I am." I advised while opening the bathroom door.

"Good. Come on in here and sit down. Keith is on the phone. He wants to give us an update about what Lynn found out from Candice."

Sitting down on the bed beside Derrick, I became attentive to what Keith was ready to explain.

"Okay Derrick and Passion. Lynn was able to catch Candice on the beach. She set up next to her and engaged in a conversation with her. Lynn stated she started off by saying how beautiful everything here is and Candice joined in. She told Lynn where she was from and that life had got hectic in her world. Candice went on to say, she needed some time away from it all. She even advised of how she was in love with a man who wasn't in love with her. Lynn said she had some regrets about somethings she had done in her life. Candice didn't give details about her regrets, but Lynn said they must be very hurtful because Candice had tears in her eyes. Lynn really feels that Candice is a hurting woman and has done a lot of wrong in her life. But Lynn also believes that she knows you all are here. When they were about to leave each other's presence. She told Lynn that she tries to keep the man she loves in reach, but there is something in her way to getting him. Candice also told her as soon as I can get it out of the way. My life could change forever." Keith said getting incredibly quiet.

"So, Keith you all believe she is talking about me?" Derrick asked.

"Yes Derrick. Lynn let Candice leave ahead of her, and she followed her back to this hotel. She is three doors down from you all. She watched her walk by you all's room door, and she stopped at the door as though she wanted to knock. Candice then went on to her room." He spoke.

"Wait Keith! Candice is only three doors down. Derrick, are you sure you didn't know she was here?" I asked staring in his eyes.

"No Passion. I did not! This all is news to me as well." Derrick responded.

"Passion don't worry. I checked with the front desk and found out she has been here for two days. She hasn't pulled any stunts yet. And plus, we are leaving before daybreak in the morning. We will be gone before she even knows it. Oh! She isn't here alone. The clerk did say there is a man accompanying her. From the description the clerk gave. I'm sure I know who that male is. The only thing I am uncertain of is, why is he with Candice? But you all don't worry about that. I will find out. Just sit tight and we will be out of here soon. If you need me or Lynn tonight. Don't hesitate to call." Keith advised.

Disconnecting the call, Derrick turned to me. "Passion, I promise I did not know she was here. And babe, I have not been messing around with her for her to say she loves me. I believe she is still holding on to the old love we shared back in high school. Please believe me!" Derrick said holding my hand.

"Derrick, please just stop! My nerves are already in an uproar. Let's just try and make the best of this night. I doubt if I get much sleep.

"I just want to lay down and see if I can." I stated.

Laying down on my right side, I turned away from Derrick. I really did not believe he was telling the truth. Therefore, I wanted to give him the cold shoulders. Derrick didn't respond back. He went to the other side of the bed and laid down. I guess we both must have been experiencing fear, because neither of us turned off the lights in the bedroom. The lights gave a sense of security. Especially since the room would not be dark. It would allow us to see anyone if they decided to come in without our permission.

After a restless night, we got up and prepared to catch our flight. Gathering our luggage, Derrick and I made sure we were not leaving anything behind. But for some reason, I had an uneasy feeling. Derrick was not saying much, and neither was I. I just kept praying silently that we get home safely. Just before walking out of the door, Derrick decided to go to the patio. Looking at him in a curious manner, I walked behind him. He stood on the patio and stared at the water.

"What is wrong? Why did you come out here?" I asked him.

"Passion, looking at the water gives me a sense of peace. I really wished that coming over here would have made our marriage better. I wanted us to heal some things and forget about others. But looking back over the last few days. Makes me think this trip was in vain. We didn't accomplish anything to regain a step in our marriage. All we accomplished was how to make our love vanish even more. Passion, when we get home. I want you to live out the rest of your life, no matter if it is with me or someone else. Tossing and turning last night, made me see what I have done in the marriage. I have been living a lie the whole time. See, I loved you in the beginning. Then my love changed as time went on. I started to view you as the same as any other woman in my life. After viewing you like this, I wanted to make you pay for what every woman had done to me. My Mom never wanted us or believed in us. She put our father before us. Aunt Shirlene took us in, but never married for trying to give us a good life. So, on occasions, she blamed us for being stuck with someone else's mistakes. Then there was my sister. Sheryl feels like she owed me her life. Therefore, she hindered me from a lot of punishments that I should have received. Maybe if I would have gone through them. I wouldn't always feel I can get away with any and everything. Let's not forget Candice. I loved her wholeheartedly, but she wanted Mr. Muncho. He had the cars, the money, and the fame at that time. Curtis was one of my best friends and she left me for him. Now she is claiming she loves me. Oh, and let us not forget Tayneshia. She made me feel as though, I could have anything I wanted at no cost. She gave me a high like a drug would give an addict. But not only did she become my addict. She became my baby mother, and a person who gave me something I can't get rid of. Then there is Stephanie on the other hand, who reminded me of you. She was soft, respectable, but she was unsure of herself. Being unsure made me use her as a get back for Candice and Marlon." Derrick explained continuing to look at the water.

With tears streaming down my face. I had to ask him just one question. "Derrick, so why did I make you hurt me? In the beginning and up until now, my love is real. I never sought out to hurt you. I gave you all my love and still do."

"Passion, you didn't hear me! I wanted to make you pay for what they did. It wasn't until I got shot that I realized your love for me. Life flashed before my eyes that day. And all God was allowing me to see was the wrong I did to you. At first, I was sorrowful. Then on other days, I was angry at you. Babe, please just take my advice and go on with your life when we get home." He said crying and holding on to my shoulders.

Staring at him, I wondered why he wanted to tell me all of this at this time. He could have waited until we arrived home. But I'm actually glad he had shared the information. It gave me a sense of direction for my life. Yes, I still love him, but I don't want to continue to be the pay back girl for other women. I've loved him from the day we started dating. The only other man I have been with besides him, is Marlon. So, he is right about one thing. I do need to take his advice. But something on the inside of me, is telling me to stay in my marriage. Only time will tell if we stay together once we get back home.

"Okay Derrick! Let's just finish this conversation on the plane and when we get home. I don't want us to be late. Keith and Lynn are downstairs waiting. Come on!" I stated as we were still standing facing each other.

"I know they are waiting, but I need to get this off my chest. I can't go another day holding this in." Derrick said as he turned back to look at the water.

"Get what off your chest? Didn't you just do that?" I asked.

"Yes, I did to a certain point. But there is much more. Last night when you were asleep. I got into your laptop and roamed through your emails. The anonymous person emailed again. This time they clarified why everything happened. They started from Tay and I cheating. Then moved on to everyone else who was involved. Whoever it is even confirmed some things that I have even been wondering about. Sheryl and Keith are really not good FBI Agents, because the information this person gave makes a whole lot of since."

"Derrick, please get to what they said. Time is ticking!" I said eagerly.

He stood quiet for a moment. Then he turned around and looked at me. Derrick was crying and staring at me as though he didn't want to share what he had found out. Walking closer to Derrick, I put my hands in his. I wanted to assure him that I would be ok to hear whatever it was. Unfortunately, before Derrick could speak another word. I heard a man's voice behind me. As I turned to see who it was, something flashed before my eyes. I felt a strong push and water splashing all around me. Did I just fall into the ocean? I can't swim! Somebody please help me! Swinging my arms and fluttering my feet, the water was bracing vastly working against me. Trying to hold my breath and squinch my eyes to see, I felt life slipping away from me. What just happened? And where is Derrick? Whose voice did I just here and what caused that flash? God, please rescue me. Is it really time for my life to end? Or will this be a form of another wake up call God is using for Derrick?

CHAPTER

17

Still feeling like I was battling for my life; I was able to see things clearer. My eyes were now popped wide open, and here I laid looking around at what appeared to be a hospital room. I started to panic as I looked at all of the machines I was hooked up to. There were wires running all over my body. After finally coming to grips with something drastic happened at the hotel in the Bahamas. I wanted to know how I got here, and where was Derrick? Is he ok? Not seeing anyone in the room with me. I pushed the nurse button on the side of the bed.

"Hello, can I help you?" The voice stated on the intercom.

"Yes, where is my husband? I need him right now!" I said getting out of breath.

"Ma'am, I will send your nurse down. Give us one moment please."

Waiting on the nurse to come into the room. I started to try and remember everything that happened. But the only thing I could remember was the flash of light. Finally, the door swung open and there stood Lynn and Keith. I kept looking behind them, hoping to see Derrick. Unfortunately, he wasn't there. This made me get nervous. Did something bad happen to him? I don't know how I'm going to take it if they say so.

"Where is Derrick?" I asked without saying anything else.

Lynn walked over closer to the bed and put her hand on my arm. "Passion, take it easy. He is ok."

"If he is ok. Why are you all here and not him?"

Keith stepped over to the bed. "He is at the police department." He stated.

"Why? Please just tell me what happened!" I said frantically.

"Passion, I guess everything will sound better coming from me." Lynn stated as she sat in the chair next to the bed. "From what Derrick stated. You all were on the patio talking about some things. When he turned around and noticed a man standing in the door entrance of you all's room. It was too late to alert you. The man had fired a shot in you all's direction. The only way to save the both of you, was to grab you and fall into the water. He said after his reaction. He started to think about how you couldn't swim. So, he started to swim under water searching for you. But he could not find you. He said he came up for air and that's when he noticed you floating in the water. He swam over to you and made it to another patio. Derrick pulled you up to safety and started to do CPR. He said he yelled for help hoping whosever patio it was, would hear him. And he was correct. The couple in the room came out and assisted him. Derrick called Keith after the paramedics came and let us know what happened. After arriving here, and we found out you would be ok. Derrick was escorted to the police department for questioning." Lynn explained in a soft voice.

"Why did he have to go for questioning? He didn't do anything wrong." I asked.

"Well Passion. Because you were unconscious, and he was the only other person to see the man." Keith responded.

"So do anyone know who this man is?" I asked.

"Yes Passion. It was Curtis Jones. Looks like he accompanied Candice to the Bahamas." Keith stated.

"Wait! So, he came to finish what he was supposed to do that day at the hotel."

Shaking his head yes. Keith said, "I guess so."

Before Lynn could speak again, the door swung open, and in walked Derrick.

"Thanks, Lynn and Keith for staying with Passion. I really appreciate it. Hey Babe! How do you feel?" Derrick asked.

"Hey Derrick! I am ok. How about you?" I asked.

"I'm good. I am only glad you are ok, and things didn't get any worse." He stated.

"So did you find out anything about why all of this happened?" I asked.

"Yes, I did! Remember before all of this happened. I was telling you about the email that was in your emails." Derrick advised. "Well, when I opened the email. I got the surprise of my life. There were pictures of Tayneshia and Candice together at different times."

"What do you mean together?" I said stunned from what he stated.

"It was not picturing of them being together sexually. These pictures look like they know each other personally, or they maybe old friends of some sort. There were also pictures of them with other people as well. And after reading the email to the entirety. I understood the pictures." Derrick explained.

"So, what did the email say?"

"The email stated that Tay and Candice are stepsisters. Seems like Tay's Father married Candice Mother about ten years ago. After Candice found out that you two were good friends. She started quizzing Tayneshia about you, and you all's relationship. Somehow Tay told Candice about her and I cheating. She even told her that you didn't have a clue about it. Tayneshia gave Candice all this information, but Candice didn't give her any about our relationship back in the day. Therefore, she was using Tay to get information on me."

"Wow! So, is there more?" I asked excited to her the information.

Derrick took a seat on the bed and continued telling what he found out in the email.

"Passion, whoever sent the email made it look like Candice was jealous of Tay and I. Therefore, she put a plan together to have us killed. In her plan she used Curtis as the hitman. He lied and told Sheryl he didn't know who hired him, but he knew the whole time." Derrick spoke.

"Ok, I understand that to a certain point. But if Curtis did not do the shooting at the Shamrock Hotel. Then who did it?"

Taking a big sigh, Derrick went on to tell the rest of the story. "Well, you were right about the adjoining doors. Candice was present in the other room. She was supposed to wait there for Curtis to come. When Curtis had arrived. He was to catch Tay and I in the act. Once he caught us. He was supposed to kill us. Unfortunately, Candice forgot she told Stephanie to meet her there. Therefore, she had to change her plans. When Stephanie got there and saw Tay and I, she started arguing with Tay. Candice listened in the other room, and when Tay went in the room, she shot her. And as soon as I walked in, she shot me. Curtis was right about one thing. When he got there, the job had been done."

"Derrick, I got all of that now. But how did they know we were over here?"

"Lynn, I think you better tell Passion the rest." Derrick said as he turned to look at Lynn.

"Ok Derrick. Passion I have a confession. Remember when I told you Marlon is a great guy." Lynn spoke softly.

"Yes Ma'am!" I answered.

"Well, I know this because, Stephanie is my daughter by my ex-husband. Because of his abusive behavior. I left him, and he kept Stephanie with him. For years, she didn't speak to me. It's been about two years now that, we have been communicating. Before Keith and I left on the trip, I called Stephanie to tell her, we were coming to the Bahamas. I also told her Keith was on an assignment. So, I guess she put two and two together because she knows Keith works for Sheryl. And since no one has saw you two. She must have thought about you all being over here. Passion, I am so sorry. I didn't know of her being involved with Candice on any level. I would have never wanted my actions to hurt anyone. Please forgive me for talking to much." Lynn explained.

Taking a deep breath, I sat in disbelief. I couldn't believe some of the stuff I was hearing. Candice was Tay's stepsister, and I never knew it. Lynn is Stephanie's mother, and I never knew that either. Everyone around me is connected somehow. I feel like an outsider for sure. And to be honest, I'm more afraid now than I was before all of this happened.

"Derrick so where are Candice and Curtis now?" I asked.

"They both have been arrested and awaiting return to Tenison" He answered.

"This is a lot of stuff to process. I would have never imagined any of this. But I've always had a suspicion that Candice was involved. She has been a nightmare for me ever since the first day I met her. Is not a surprise to me that she wanted me dead. I'm just glad God was protecting me. Oh yeah! Lynn I can see the resemblance in facial features between you and Stephanie now. I just hate that her heart does not resemble yours as well. And I totally understand how she could have been angry at you. She must have thought you abandoned her when you left your husband. I'm also glad that you all had a chance to bond after all these years. It's nothing like having your mother there for you. So, Lynn I'm not angry about you sharing with your daughter. And plus, no one can blame someone else for another person's actions. To tell you all the truth, I am just ready to get home. Hopefully, when we get back home. We can all try to live our lives to the fullest without all the drama. Oh, by the way! Did anyone let Marlon know what happened? I would hate for him to be at the airport waiting on all of us." I spoke.

Keith spoke up, "Yes, I called him."

We continued to conversate about the outs and ins of everything that has happened. Getting more information has cleared up a lot of the unanswered questions we all had. But what is still left unanswered is, who is the anonymous person. How do they know all of this and how are they involved?

"Yes, Passion. I totally agree with you about getting home. I want to get on with our lives as well." Derrick reiterated.

"Passion and Derrick! Have you all decided to stay together?" Lynn asked.

Looking over at me with a smirk on his face, Derrick stated," Ma'am that is not up to me!"

"Well Passion. That leaves the answer up to you." Keith uttered.

Searching for the right words. I looked at each person in the room. I wasn't sure within myself right now. Therefore, providing an answer would basically be a lie. But instead of telling the truth right now. I gave them what I knew they wanted to hear. Floating in my head was the words I remember Derrick stating to me before. He said that I could not handle the truth, and right now, I don't see them handling my truth either.

"Well! We will just have to see after we get home. So much has happened, and I hate to give an answer to something that only time can provide." I explained.

"Passion you are absolutely correct. I want you and Derrick to know. If y'all are going to stay together. You both must work at it and leave everything and everyone else behind. That's the only way a marriage can work!" Lynn advised.

Keith nodded his head in agreement and then stated that as soon as the doctors released me. We would be going home. He had received a message from Sheryl about everything, and she said it was clear for us to leave. Just when he finished telling us the good news. The doctor walked in.

"Hello everyone. Mrs. Wilson, I have great news. Everything came back fine. You are free to leave. There is only one thing you will need to do." The doctor advised.

"Thank God! And what is it that I need to do, Sir?" I asked.

"It is nothing urgent. You will need to follow up with your primary doctor in about two weeks. You can show them the discharge papers and they should be able to recheck you according to that information. I have submitted your discharge papers and the nurse should be here in a moment." He stated.

The doctor had brought great news. We can now prepare to get on with our lives. After the doctor left. The nurse came straight in behind him. She unhooked everything and gave me my discharge papers. Excited about my release. I turned to Derrick for him to assist me with getting up. Due to the pressure of falling in the water, and the compressions Derrick used in CPR. My body was sore in different areas. I'm sure glad the nurse was observant and insisted on escorting me to a cab. Once we made it to the airport, I felt so relieved about everything. I recall being nervous about coming to the Bahamas, and now I'm excited about leaving it. The scenery was beautiful like I imagined it. But under the circumstances. I really don't see me coming back here for a long time.

We all boarded our flights and enjoyed the quiet flight home. Derrick fell asleep just like the last time, and I listened to music. Lynn and Keith sat in front of us. They seemed to be having some meaningful conversations, because the looks on their faces told it all. It will not be long now, until I can really see if we will stay trapped in this marriage. Or will we leave it and move on. Only the man above has the answer to that. All Derrick and I can do is speculate on our marriage because we both still have feelings for other people.

CHAPTER

18

Looking out the window, I saw the Tenison water tower. This let me know that we were about to land. I never felt so excited to be back in Tenison. All I can think about is home sweet home. I was not even thinking about the problems we left behind, or the problems we are bringing back. I just wanted to get off the plane and go straight to our home.

"Well Passion. We are home. Let's go face what we left here." Derrick stated.

"Yes Derrick. Are you ready? Because I sure am." I said with enthusiasm.

Exiting the airplane was much easier this time. We knew the procedures and we were awfully familiar with the airport. Walking into the entrance I started to look for Marlon. Deep down inside I was excited to see him. Unfortunately, things once again had been changed without my knowledge.

"Is Marlon still picking us up? I asked.

"No Passion. I'm sorry! I forgot to tell you Sheryl would be picking us up." Derrick explained.

"Is there something wrong?"

"No, it is not. Marlon had something to come up. Since our departure time had to change. He could not be there at the time of our arrival. Passion you look disappointed." He said in a joking manner.

"No! I'm not. I was thinking he was the designated person that's all."

Walking on ahead of Derrick. I saw Sheryl standing closely by the door. She had a peculiar look on her face.

"Hello Sheryl. How are you?" I spoke.

"I'm great. The real question is, how are you?" She responded.

"I am ok. Only glad to be home." I advised.

"Well, that's awesome. Are y'all ready?" Sheryl asked.

Derrick responded, "Yes, we are. Oh! Keith and Lynn said to let you know that we can go on. They are being picked up by Keith's business partner." Derrick stated.

Thinking outside of the box. I thought about Marlon telling me that he and Keith were business partners. So, does that mean Marlon is picking them up? And why did he tell Derrick he couldn't do the same for us? Or is Derrick not telling me the truth. For some reason, I'm feeling a little paranoid. Especially, since Derrick said that Marlon had something to come up. I guess I should not be feeling this way without any proof. All I can do is pray silently for God to cover me at all costs.

We got in Sheryl's car and started on our journey home. Derrick rode in the front with her, and I rode in the back seat. Looking up at the rearview mirror, I noticed Sheryl looking back at me. Our eyes met. She was looking at me in a way that put me on edge. I turned my head to break the stare we had became engaged in. I guess this is what made her move on whatever thoughts that were radiating in her head.

"Passion, I have already spoken with Derrick about the shooting at the Shamrock Hotel. Now, I need to speak with you regarding it." She spoke.

"Okay, but why? Is there something Derrick forgot to tell me? I asked.

"Uhhh! I'm not quite sure what part he told you. But the part I am concerned with is, the part that includes you." Sheryl said twitching her right eye up.

"Sheryl! Stop it! I told you to just let it go. Candice and Curtis are being brought back here for all that has happened." Derrick advised Sheryl.

"Derrick! What is Sheryl talking about?" I asked.

"Passion, Nothing!" He answered looking in Sheryl's direction.

Continuing to drive with an angry look on her face. Sheryl got quiet for a moment, but then she started the conversation back up.

"Passion, Derrick doesn't want me to bring up what we discovered in relevance to you in this case. But I feel you need to know. I totally understand why you did what you did, but there is no excuse for it. Answer one question for me? Did you shoot Derrick and Tay?" Sheryl asked.

Shocked at what Sheryl has just asked me. I looked in her direction. A part of me wanted to answer, Hell yes for all they have done to me! But the other part of me spoke out and denied the allegations. Sheryl looked as though she did not believe anything I said, and I could feel the hostility spirit that had set up in the atmosphere of the car. She drove faster than she usually drives, and Derrick looked out the car window looking disgusted. I couldn't understand where all this was coming from. Derrick didn't want Sheryl to share what she thought. But for some reason, I wanted to hear her thoughts.

"Sheryl, I'm not sure of what you think you know. But I'm willing to listen and answer what parts are correct." I explained.

"Passion! Can you and Sheryl just leave well enough alone? It's done now and we cannot change anything. Why cause more harm to our marriage?" Derrick yelled.

"Derrick, I understand how you feel. But the truth needs to be heard. I already told you if she confesses to it. I won't tell what I know." She stated strongly.

We had arrived at our house. Sheryl had parked the car in the driveway and sat looking at Derrick. Sitting in the backseat, I spoke out to them both.

"Sheryl, you are correct! The truth does need to be told. Therefore, can we get our things out of the car first, and go into the house. I will be glad to answer any questions you may have. But I am not sure if you all are ready to hear my answers."

We all gathered our things and proceeded into the house. Sitting our things in the hallway, I walked into the den. Derrick and Sheryl followed me. I guess they figured out that I was ready to talk about everything. Despite Sheryl saying she had questions for me. I spoke out before she could spit out one word.

"So, you want to know did I shoot Tay and Derrick? Well Sheryl, here it goes. I knew about them cheating with each other for two years now. The anonymous person didn't just start emailing. She has been doing it for a couple of years. She started out with just sending pictures of Derrick and Tay meeting locations. Then she graduated to sending pictures of messages. Therefore, I started watching Derrick's actions and movement. Once I confirmed it. I just sat back and tried to keep calm about it. I prayed that it would stop just like the others stopped. But when it didn't. I started to plan my attack and I wanted my attack to bring me satisfaction. I loved Derrick with all my heart and gave up my life for him. I moved here against my mother's wishes. She had explained to me that Derrick didn't love me the way I loved him. Sheryl, I know you feel where I am coming from, because you watched your husband cheat on you too. But have you ever watched him cheat repeatedly? There have been times I've stood off and watched him sex them better than he does me. I have sat in my car and watch him wine and dine them better than he does me. I have taken him beating me when they didn't give him what he wanted. He has verbally degraded me. But I still love him. I lost my fight as a woman and was only fighting for someone who wasn't fighting for me. See, I've have been trying to overlook him cheating for years. But when he cheated with the one person, I thought had my back. I was done! How could she do this to me? I shared everything about Derrick and me with her. She knew how much I loved him. Hell, I loved her more than I loved my own sister. I even loved her enough to not tell her that I knew she was the anonymous person. So, I let her think I didn't know who she was. Because by doing this, she would always send me information I could use to track them. The day of the shooting she decided to call the house instead of emailing. So, I took Derrick's gun and placed it in my purse. When he said he was leaving for work. I left too. I knew he was lying about work because I already knew Tay had reserved both rooms. I guess she did this so no one would be in the room next to them. When I arrived at the hotel. I met one of the housekeepers who work there, and she let me into the room. Tayneshia was very dumb. She never checked the other room. She just always uses their favorite room. Which happened to be room 132. Therefore, it was easy for me to slip into the room. I waited in the other room. When Derrick and Tay arrived, I heard people talking. I looked out the room and saw Tay and Stephanie arguing. So, I waited patiently and gathered my strength to overcome the fear within me. When Derrick advised Tay to go into the room my adrenaline was flowing. I came from out the closet and shot her. She did not have time to run due to the first shot went into her chest. It knocked her backwards on to the bed. Once I pulled the trigger. I could not stop myself. I just kept shooting. I wanted to make sure she was dead. With each shot, I thought about every time I watched them have sex. The more I thought about that, the eager I got to do Derrick the same way. I then went in the bathroom to wait on Derrick. Once he came in, I stepped back out. I pulled the trigger one more time, but it got stuck. Derrick immediately raced over to me, and we started tussling over the gun. Then the gun went off and he fell backwards onto the floor. I was so nervous that I fell on the floor beside him. I began to shake and yell his name. Realizing what I had just done, I became hysterical. Calming myself down by rocking back and forth. I touched Derrick one more time. Finally, Derrick opened his eyes and told me to get out of there. He advised me to go home and clean myself up. Derrick also told me not to say a word to anyone about what happened. He would take care of it. So, I left Sheryl." I stated with tears gushing out of my eyes.

Sheryl's face was full of tears as well. She sat quietly for a moment and then she stated, "Derrick you knew this the whole time and you just let me tell you what I thought I knew?"

"Yes Sheryl! I'm sorry! But I have caused so much hurt to so many people my whole life, that I didn't want to hurt Passion anymore. I drove her to commit murder, all because she loves me. Sheryl, please let this go." He advised.

"Derrick, have you forgot someone died!" She spoke.

"No, I haven't. But Candice did have plans to kill us first. Did you forget that? And plus, Candice did hire Curtis as well. He just didn't get the chance to carry it out on Tayneshia and I. But he followed through on it in the Bahamas in which Passion was hurt." Derrick yelled.

Sheryl turned to me and stated, "So Passion. You knew it was Tay emailing you right?"

"Yes, because I used a system at work to look up anonymous emails. It gave me all of her information." I advised.

"Okay. So do you know who is sending the emails now?" She asked.

"At first, I thought it was Tay's sister Janelle. But after learning Candice is her stepsister in the Bahamas. I believe it could be her."

"Correct! That's who I was thinking now too." Sheryl agreed.

"Sis will you please do me this last favor! Don't turn Passion in. No matter if she believes me or not. I love her and I don't want her to go to jail." Derrick explained.

Sheryl hesitated and then spoke, "I'm not going to say anything, but you both got to promise me one thing."

"And just what is that?" I asked.

"That you all will stay together and live happily ever after!" She insisted on saying with a smile on her face.

Looking at Sheryl I tried to keep a straight face. But unfortunately, I could not. With a mountain full of tears in my eyes. I spoke these words. "Speaking on my behalf. I cannot guarantee you that Sheryl. Yes, I still love your brother. But I must admit I love myself more now. Going to the Bahamas and meeting Lynn gave me hope for my life. For years, I didn't love myself, and I was just existing in life. I was insecure about my beauty, my size, and my intelligence. All because of how your brother cheated on me. I did everything a woman was supposed to do in a marriage. So, I thought! I cooked, cleaned, worked, and even tried to do the inevitable in the bed. Let alone, I prayed over him, prayed for him, and thanked God for him being my husband. But did that stop him. Hell no, it didn't! Sheryl, what's so bad about it is. I loved him enough to kill for him. Now someone's mother, sister, wife, and child are gone. Not to mention, Derrick had a child outside of our marriage, and he is HIV positive. But through it all, God still has granted me deliverance. He didn't let my test come back positive. I walked away from falling in an ocean of water, and I can't even swim. Therefore, I would be wrong to make you that promise. Derrick and I are far from living a happily ever after life. So, if you must turn me in. Do what you must do! Because as sure as my name is Passion Wilson. I am taking the right steps this time. I will be first in my life, and the man who accompanies me will put me first."

Before I could continue speaking. The doorbell rang. We all looked at one another in shock. We had just arrived home and we were not expecting any company. Therefore, Derrick got up and went to answer the door. Sheryl and I remained seated waiting to hear who may be at the door. Unfortunately, we didn't hear one word. This brought on some worries in my mind of who it could be. Was it Marlon? Or maybe it was Keith and Lynn? And God forbid it to be Stephanie or Candice. But whoever it was, knew we were home. Derrick was taking so long to come back, that I got up to go see what was going on. Only to walk up on his body lying in the front door entrance with blood pouring out of his chest. I couldn't move. I just let off a scream of horror. Sheryl came running to the door. She jumped over his body and ran outside. I knelt in shock and watched the blood run from his body. Derrick just stared at me without saying one word. I was having flashbacks of the day at the hotel. Derrick's body reminded me of when I shot Tay. As I looked at him. All I saw was how her body fell backwards from all the shots. He landed in the same position with the same wounds as Tay. Derrick must have known I was in a trance because he moved his hand toward my face, but before it made contact. I grabbed his hand and held it tightly.

"Passion. Always remember I didn't set out to hurt you. I love you and always will. Babe, live your life now. But can you do me one favor? Please make sure Lenton is taken care of?" He said as his eyes began to roll back and forth.

"Babe, I will do whatever you want. Just don't leave me. I take back what I said earlier. I do love you. We can make this work. Please hang on!" I said dropping tears onto his arm.

Sheryl came back in and joined us on the floor. Breathing hard she uttered out," Hang on bro! I got help on the way. Stay strong! You can make it!"

"Did you catch him?" Derrick asked.

"Catch him? Did you see who it was, Derrick?" Sheryl asked as she pushed on his body to get his attention.

Derrick was drifting in and out. We tried to keep him attentive until help could arrive.

"Babe, did you hear Sheryl? Did you see who shot you?" I said crying.

Derrick opened his eyes wide and looked at the both of us. He turned to Sheryl first and said he loved her. Then he turned to me and said the same. Before he closed his eyes back. He looked at me and tried to say something. His mouth was moving, but there was nothing coming out of it. Derrick's head slowly drifted to the left. He started shallow breathing, and I felt his pulse declining in his hand. I couldn't believe this was actually happening even though, I tried to make it happen myself. The man I love is really leaving me, and there is nothing I can do about it. I couldn't even say a word. I just looked at Sheryl hoping she could save him like before. With no other options at this point. I started to pray.

"Father who is in heaven,

We are here lifting Derrick up to you. God turn it around. Don't let this be the end result. Heal him please, Lord! I know you as a provider. Grant me this favor, God. I'm pleading with you right now. Help us Lord! I believe he shall live and not die! Amen." I shouted holding Derrick and Sheryl's hand.

After praying. I hope God heard me. We never think about losing someone forever, until the process begins. Evidently, Candice and Curtis weren't the only ones that wanted Derrick dead. They are supposedly still in the Bahamas in jail. Who has the nerve to come to our home and do this? How did they know he would answer the door?

Sheryl and I continued to keep Derrick attentive by calling his name loudly. Finally, the emergency responders arrived, and started procedures to save him. After repeated attempts, they loaded him in the ambulance to transport him to the hospital. Watching them drive away, Sheryl immediately advised me to get my things so we could go to the hospital. Grabbing my purse. I followed Sheryl's instructions, but not before going into the bedroom to check the security cameras. I explained to Sheryl that I needed to use the restroom first. In a hurry, I rewinded the camera and there he was. The man who shot Derrick. He stood about six feet. He had a mocha complexion and was well built. But what I noticed first, was the wedding band on his hand as he pointed the gun at Derrick. It was the same one Derrick described to the police officer. Wow! How could I have been so stupid.

"Passion come on! Hurry up! We need to go." Sheryl yelled.

"Here I come! I'm sorry! I was so nervous that it just kept flowing." I answered.

We left the house and headed to the hospital. Sheryl put her foot to the gas petal, and we made it in record time. Running in the hospital, I got the strangest feeling. After arriving to the help desk. I understood why. Derrick had died on his way to the hospital. It was official. The man I loved is no longer in his earthly body. God did not hear my prayer. Derrick has left me. Ever since I started to plan my attack for Tay and Derrick. I always wondered how I would feel if he died. Now, I know how. A part of me feels empty. Once again, I am defeated in my life.

Walking into the holding room, my feelings were all over the place. I became sad and then I was happy. How could one have so many emotions about one's death. I stared at him wishing he would open his eyes and say something. I began to rub his face when I notice Sheryl staring at me.

"Sheryl, are you ok?" I asked.

"Yes! But are you ok? Passion you can put on for everyone else. But I know you love my brother." She explained.

"I think I'm ok. My mind is telling me I am ok, but my body is ready to drop to the floor. Sheryl, how can he leave me this way? You're right about me trying to be a tough girl on the outside. But on the inside, I'm falling apart." I spoke crying.

"Passion, I guess we don't have to worry about what happened at the Shamrock hotel now after all. Seems like whoever really wanted him dead succeeded. My little brother is really gone, and I couldn't save him this time. You said he left you. No! He left us. I've lived my whole life trying to make sure he was ok. And the one time he needed me. I wasn't there, and I was just a room away." She said sobbing.

We embraced and comforted each other before exiting the room. Walking down the hallway I noticed a tall black figure of a man. He was dressed in blue jeans, a black hoodie, and black tennis shoes. The man was speaking with the clerk. I couldn't see his face at the moment. But as we got closer, I saw the ring on his finger. It was the same black and silver band Derrick spoke of the day the officer came by. It also was the band I saw on our security cameras at home. I became extremely nervous. I can't believe he has the audacity to come to the hospital. Did he forget about what he has done? Or just maybe he has come to make sure the job was completed. Whatever his reasons maybe. I don't want to see him right now. The closer Sheryl and I got to the man. The more fear mustard up within me. I began shaking and Sheryl noticed it.

"Passion are you ok?" She asked.

Just before I was about to speak. The man turned around and faced us. Without a shadow of a doubt, he was exactly who I thought he was. My eyes grew, my mouth dropped opened, and my legs went numb. Sheryl tried breaking my fall but was unsuccessful. Therefore, I collapsed on the floor and passed out. All I could hear were voices of people calling my name. Darkness was all I could see, and in my mind, I was answering them that I was ok. Unfortunately, they couldn't hear me. But the one voice I could hear clearly was the voice of the man that I know killed my husband.

The End